To Sandra —

KISS ME IN THE MOONLIGHT

A KISS ME ROMANTIC SUSPENSE

Happy reading!

Lindzee Armstrong

"The world is a book, and those who do not travel read only one page."
-St. Augustine

Cover Design by Steven Novak
Interior Design by Snowflake Press
Edited by Red Adept Editing and CookieLynn Publishing Services

Tooele, UT
Print ISBN 978-0-9981667-3-5
Library of Congress Control Number 2017907385

USA TODAY BESTSELLING AUTHOR

LINDZEE ARMSTRONG

KISS ME IN THE MOONLIGHT

A KISS ME ROMANTIC SUSPENSE

CHAPTER ONE

Two months ago, when Paige had first imagined how her summer would play out, it hadn't been anything like this. She looked around the tiny breakfast room, anticipation ricocheting through her stomach. Her fingers curled around the straps of her drawstring backpack as her heart thrummed loudly in her chest.

Belgium. She couldn't believe she was actually on the Battlefield of Europe. She'd pored over first-hand accounts of the Thirty Year's War, examined primary source material surrounding the French Revolution, and extensively studied the effects of World War I and II on Europe as a whole. Now she'd get to see the places she'd spent a lifetime learning about.

Paige inhaled a shaky breath. When she arrived at the hotel last night, her eyes had been so bleary with jet lag that she'd been unable to take it all in. Now, she looked eagerly around the space. The breakfast room was quaint, with four round tables big enough for six around the area. Faded gold and green wallpaper, dotted with fleurs-de-lis, covered the walls. Mismatched chairs circled each table, making Paige feel like she was in her father's dining room. Except this was Belgium, not Washington, D.C.

The room held a trio of elderly tourists sporting fanny packs, despite the early morning hour. A young boy spoke excitedly in what sounded like Italian as his mother laughed and tried to quiet him. But it was the woman sitting alone at the third table who caught Paige's eye. She had creamy skin sprinkled with the lightest dusting of freckles, and looked close to Paige's age—maybe twenty-five or twenty-six.

Paige tried to peer inconspicuously without being obvious. The silky dark chocolate hair with a fringe of bangs matched the photo she'd been given of Layla, but she didn't want to assume and end up looking like an idiot.

She'd get breakfast and hope the woman noticed her and spoke up. Paige picked her way through the tables, heading to the buffet along the far wall. The heady aroma of unfamiliar breads mixed with fresh fruit made her stomach growl. What time had her fellow coworkers arrived last night? Paige had hoped she'd get to meet Layla, Tyler, and Eddie before meeting the twenty high schoolers they'd spend the next nineteen days guiding through Europe. By summer's end, they'd have guided four such tours.

Paige grabbed a porcelain plate and eyed the foods spread out before her. A basket of rolls sat at one end of the table, with a platter of deli meats and unfamiliar cheeses next to it. A large bowl of something white and creamy—yogurt, maybe?—was next to a selection of fruit. The hand-painted plaque above the table declared *Breakfast is served daily from six a.m. to nine a.m.* in French, German, Dutch, and English.

She hoped her French would be up to the task of communicating with natives this summer. The private schools she'd attended in Washington, D.C. had strong French language programs. But this was different. Her accent would probably give her away as as soon as she opened her mouth.

Paige glanced at the woman with chocolate brown hair. She was absorbed in her phone and hadn't noticed Paige. Maybe it wasn't Layla, but just someone who looked like her.

Paige placed a little of everything on her plate. She grabbed something at the very end that she hoped was jam. At the table, the woman brushed her hair back, exposing more of her face. The thin nose and heart-shaped face matched the picture Paige had studied on the plane ride over.

She should go say hello and ask if she could sit by Layla. It would be a long three months if she didn't make any friends. Even Europe could be lonely if she let it.

Paige's fingers curled around her plate, her stomach swooping as she drew closer. The girl looked up and offered a smile. Definitely Layla.

"Hi," Paige said. "Is this spot taken?"

Layla shook her head, making her stick-straight hair bounce across her shoulders. "Nope. Please, save me from eating alone."

"Thanks." Paige slid into the chair in relief, setting her backpack on the floor by her feet.

"You must be Paige. I recognize you from your photo," Layla said.

"I am. And you're Layla."

"That's me." Her voice had a musical quality to it that instantly made Paige feel grungy in comparison. "It's nice to finally meet you. Is this your first trip with Destiny Tours?"

"Yes." When her mentor professor, Dr. Hodges, had told her about the job, she'd been hesitant. Three months in Europe, all expenses paid. Free admission to the best museums in the world. It all sounded like a dream, and she should've jumped at the chance instead of being reluctant. But the last year had been hard.

"You're falling behind," Dr. Hodges had gently reminded her. "Your grades were barely average last semester. This is a good opportunity to correct course.

4

You'll need to start writing your dissertation in the fall. This is the perfect research opportunity."

"I don't know." Paige fiddled with a lock of hair and thought of the man who had broken her heart. What if he returned to D.C., and she was gone?

"It'll give you some great experience before you start teaching," Dr. Hodges had prodded. "The hiring board loves hands-on experience."

So Paige had agreed to the summer in Europe. Dr. Hodges had written her a glowing recommendation, and she'd gotten the job.

"I worked with Destiny Tours last summer," Layla said, pulling Paige out of the past. "Best experience of my life. You're going to love it."

Paige had no doubt she'd love Europe. The teenagers she'd be chaperoning? That was the part that made her nervous. "How difficult is the job?" Paige asked, hoping the apprehension didn't leak through her voice.

Layla shrugged. "Not bad. Were you ever a residence adviser for freshmen?"

"No." With her father's brownstone a mere ten-minute walk from campus, it hadn't made financial sense to move out. And she'd always worked as a professor's assistant, eager to learn as much as she could.

"Oh. Well, it's a lot like that. Lots of energy and lots of fun. We usually run the kids so ragged during the day that they're too exhausted for evening shenanigans."

That was something, at least.

"So, Paige, where are you from?" Layla asked.

"Washington, D.C."

"Oooo, really? Is your father a senator or something?"

Paige laughed. "No, nothing like that. He's a history professor at Georgetown. He specializes in American studies."

"Wow, that's so cool. Did you attend Georgetown, then?"

Paige took a sip of her orange juice, nearly gagging on all the pulp. Yuck. "Yes. I'm working on my PhD right now. I've got a job waiting for me in my dad's department as soon as I graduate."

"Wow." Layla leaned back in her chair, eyebrows raised and eyes wide. "I'm going to feel like an idiot next to you. I barely managed to get my bachelors."

"What did you study?" Paige asked politely.

"Mostly sleeping in and talking my way out of failing." Layla smirked. "School isn't really my thing."

Great. Paige hoped she wouldn't end up chaperoning a chaperone. Talk about flighty.

"Have you had a chance to meet the guys yet?" Paige asked.

"I ran into Tyler last night. Apparently Eddie broke his foot last week and had to quit. Tyler wasn't sure who they'd found as a replacement."

"That really stinks," Paige said. As resistant as she'd been to the job at first, now that she was here, she couldn't imagine having to quit.

"I feel bad for Mr. Dawson. It can't have been easy finding a replacement on such short notice."

"I'm sure he had qualified applicants lined up at his door. This is an incredible opportunity."

"Can't argue with that." Layla's phone rang. "Sorry, I've got to take this. I'll just be a moment."

Paige nodded, and Layla walked out of the room. Paige fished the information packet from her backpack. She'd gone through it a dozen times on the flight over, but one more wouldn't hurt.

Twenty teenagers—Paige hadn't been in a room with that many kids since high school.

You're only twenty-six, her father had reminded her when she voiced her concerns. But high school felt like a lifetime ago. Growing up as the only child of a widower, she'd spent most of her time interacting with other adults—mainly professors at Georgetown. She never quite knew what to do with the younger crowd.

"That was Tyler," Layla said, sliding into her chair. "He and the new guy are going to meet us down here. I thought we could have a quick meeting before the kids start arriving from the airport. They'll trickle in throughout the day."

"Sounds great," Paige said. Maybe Layla wasn't as flighty as she first thought. "So, who's the new guy?"

Layla shrugged. "Nick something-or-other. Guess we'll find out soon."

Nick. The name instantly conjured images of stolen kisses in the moonlight, the taste of cinnamon on her tongue and fire racing through her veins.

She pushed the images away, locking them carefully behind the door labeled *do not remember*. Nick was a common enough name. Not every Nick was a no-good scumbag. They didn't all disappear in the middle of the night without so much as a goodbye. She shouldn't let four letters, strung together in a most unfortunate way, prejudice her against a colleague she'd spend the next three months with.

"Oh, here they are," Layla said, raising a hand.

Two men stood in the doorway, their stances relaxed. One was tall and gangly, with a thin face, freckled skin, and dishwater blond hair. And the other—

Paige's breath caught. He carried himself with a confidence she'd always envied, hands tucked into the pockets of denim jeans that hugged him like a glove. His hair was a little longer than it had been two months ago, but a beard still shadowed his strong jawline. She could almost feel it rubbing against the sensitive flesh of her cheeks as those strong arms held her close.

No. No, no, no, no, no. This had to be some sort of cruel joke.

He scanned the room, as though sensing her stare. Had he thought about her even once since leaving? His eyes found hers. They were still a startling emerald, even from here.

His eyebrows raised in surprise, but he schooled his face into a careful mask.

Her hands tightened on the information packet as a knot tied itself in her stomach. What on earth was Mr. Dawson thinking, hiring someone like Nick?

Layla made a noise, almost like a purr, in the back of her throat. "New guy is *hot*."

Heart breaker, more like it. Paige's chest tightened as Nick strode toward her, his steps unsure for the first time. Good. He should be scared to face her.

Layla rose, holding out her hand. "You must be Nick."

"Yes. It's nice to meet you," he said. Paige stayed rooted to her chair, frozen.

Nick. In Brussels.

"Paige, this is Tyler," Layla said.

Paige gave a curt nod. Tyler's face flushed, and he and Nick both took their chairs.

"Hi," Nick said, his voice a soft caress that had her shivering. "Wow. This is the last place I expected to see you."

She self-consciously brushed a strand of copper-colored hair behind one ear. She wanted to say something biting and caustic, but her mouth was a desert incapable of speech.

Snatches of the past flashed through her mind. Reading the email in disbelief. Rushing to his apartment, only to find it empty. Dialing his number and realizing it had been disconnected.

Layla looked back and forth between them, her darkly penciled brows pulled down in confusion. "Do you two know each other?"

"In a manner of speaking," Paige choked out. She'd been falling for Nick—maybe even in love with him. She'd thought he felt the same way.

Nick leaned back in his chair, his green eyes darkening with an emotion she couldn't decipher. "We used to date."

Layla whipped her gaze back and forth between them, her mouth forming a surprised *o*. "What a . . . coincidence," she stammered.

"Where did you go?" Paige said, the words barely a whisper. The question had plagued her for months. The email had been only three short lines, offering no information.

Nick flexed his fingers. "An opportunity came up that I couldn't refuse. I thought sudden would be best."

Sudden was a whirlwind kiss goodbye and an empty apartment by the weekend. What Nick had done was something else.

"I thought I'd at least rate a phone call," she said, trying to infuse anger into her tone. "Guess I was wrong."

"I am sorry about that." His eyes were soft and sincere. He folded his arms, and she tried not to stare at his bulging biceps. But he offered no further explanation.

"Unbelievable," she muttered. "How did you get this job, anyway?"

"I'm friends with Don. He asked me to fill in when Eddie broke his foot."

Paige's back stiffened as her fingers curled into her palms. "Wait—you didn't even have to apply?"

Nick shifted, scooting closer. "Don was in a bind, and I agreed to help him out."

"Maybe we should go." Layla rose, and Tyler followed suit.

Paige clamped a hand around Layla's arm. "Please, stay. You mentioned a meeting before the kids get here."

"Right." Layla's tone was still uneasy.

"So let's start discussing," Paige said.

Tyler put a hand to his mouth, his shoulders hunched, and eyes hooded. "So we have twenty teens on this one, right, Layla? Eight boys and twelve girls?"

"Yes. They range in age from fifteen to eighteen . . ."

But Paige was barely listening. How was she supposed to spend the next three months in Nick's presence? She'd spent the last two trying to forget him and their four-month-long intense relationship.

She tried to focus as Layla talked about who would be responsible for what, and the best way to make the summer run smoothly. But all Paige could do was stare at Nick, who stared back, his mesmerizing emerald eyes making her stomach churn.

"And I think that's it," Layla said. "Kids will trickle in throughout the morning. Paige and I will help with check-in here at reception. You boys stick close to the hotel and answer any questions that may arise while Paige and I are busy. We'll have a welcome meeting first thing in the morning, then spend three days exploring Belgium before the bus leaves for Colmar."

Tyler and Layla bolted from the room as soon as she was finished speaking, obviously eager to escape the tension radiating off Nick and Paige.

Paige rose as well, ready to make a quick escape, but a warm hand caught her arm and held.

"Can we talk?" Nick asked, his eyes pleading.

For a moment, she almost agreed—wanted to agree. But she forced herself to shake off his arm. "I have nothing to say to you," she said stiffly.

This time, she'd be the one to walk away.

CHAPTER TWO

It took all of Nick's agency training to keep his stance unconcerned and face relaxed as he watched Paige walk out of the breakfast room. Her hips swayed in a way that made his mouth water and heart ache. She'd crashed into his life like a tidal wave, upending all his carefully laid plans. He'd been only too willing to let it happen.

And then he'd got the call. Another mission—one that had the potential of lasting months. Disappearing had seemed like his best—and only—option. He'd felt himself falling, and it had terrified him. Better to cut ties.

Had Don known that this Paige was his Paige? Nick ran a hand through his hair, the possibility making his stomach sink. She wasn't supposed to ever see him again. She didn't deserve the complications a life with him would bring.

One table over, a trio of elderly tourists spoke loudly in Mandarin about the sites they were most excited to see. The bus boy carefully cleared the mom and son's table of plates while humming a popular American song off-key. A bell on the door in the front lobby jingled, the heavy footsteps that accompanied it indicating a man had entered the hotel.

Nick glanced at his watch. Three minutes had passed—enough time for Paige to escape to her room. He grabbed an apple, biting into it without tasting the crisp, sweet flavor. Years of training had taught him to eat when he could, whether he wanted to or not. He never knew when the next meal would come while out in the field.

He had to call Don. If this was some trick, Nick had half a mind to leave right now. Being back in Europe made him edgy, like there was an itch he couldn't quite find to scratch. Having Paige thrust on him so unexpectedly intensified the feeling. Nothing had felt right since he'd gotten the call two months ago and headed to Amsterdam for a mission that resulted in his partner's death.

Nick headed to the stairwell, years of practice keeping his pace leisurely so as not to draw attention, despite his desire to run. As soon as the door swung shut behind him, he took the stairs two at a time.

The bedroom was empty. Tyler must've disappeared with Layla. Nick couldn't blame him for trying to escape the crushing tension. Two twin beds were crammed into the space, and a tiny desk had been stuffed into a corner. At least this bedroom had a private bathroom. He'd stayed in his fair share of hotels that had one communal washroom for the entire floor.

Paige had talked endlessly about her desire to tour Europe. He'd wanted to tell her how wonderful it was—the way history seemed to ooze from the cobblestone and bricks. But Paige only knew his cover story. It would've been hard to explain why an accountant had spent so much time in Europe without seeing any of the typical tourist sites.

He was glad she'd finally made it here. Hopefully his presence didn't ruin her summer. The last thing he wanted was to hurt her more than he already had.

There was still time to disappear before the tour officially began tomorrow. He could go home to his sparsely furnished apartment in Virginia and resume his research. He had a few contacts at the agency who might be willing to help.

But everything had gone wrong in Europe. It was why he'd come back, despite his hesitations.

He'd talk to Don before making any decisions.

Nick shrugged into a jacket, then grabbed his laptop. The holster of his gun pressed against the small of his back, a comforting and constant presence. They might've made him turn in his badge—put him on suspension until the higher-ups could determine his fate—but he still had his weapon. He had the heart of an agent.

Outside, he found a small park right across the street from the hotel. Trees shaded the dirt pathways, allowing light to filter through and warm the air. The smell of damp dirt filled his nostrils as he entered the small sanctuary. An older gentleman walked past with a dog on his leash, but otherwise, the area was quiet.

Nick picked a bench, settling in. Time to call Don.

The phone clicked on mid-ring. "Hello?" Don's voice was high and a little effeminate. Nick could almost see him sitting at his kitchen table in silk pajamas, sipping a cup of coffee as he perused the paper. The guys had teased him mercilessly during agency training. Nick hadn't been surprised when Don turned in his badge after only a year, moved to England, and started Destiny Tours.

"Paige is here," Nick said, making his voice as rough as razor blades. "That wasn't part of the deal, Don."

"Paige?" He sounded genuinely confused.

"Paige Eldredge." The sound of her name cut like a knife. "If I'd known she was one of the chaperones, I never would've come. But you knew that, didn't you?"

"If you're going to yell at me, fine." Don's voice was even and unruffled. "But at least tell me what I've done wrong, so that I can feel properly chastised."

Nick frowned, listening to the nuance of Don's tone, checking for any hint of deception. Was it possible that Don really hadn't known who Paige was? Nick flashed back to the last six months of conversation with his friend. He'd mentioned he was dating someone from D.C. Don knew that a mission had effectively ended the relationship. But it wasn't like Nick had gone on and on about her.

"Paige—the chaperone you hired for this trip."

"Yes?" Don said, his tone polite.

"She's *the* Paige—the one I dated in D.C. The one I dumped in an email."

"Oh." Don's voice rose, and Nick could imagine him pushing away the paper as he sat straighter in his chair. "Oh. I'm so sorry. I had no idea."

"If you're lying to me—"

"I'm not. I think you did tell me her name was Paige, and of course I knew she was in D.C. But I never imagined I was hiring the same girl."

"Why did you hire her?"

"She's a PhD student at Georgetown. Her letter of recommendation was impeccable. I would've been an idiot not to."

Nick knew that Don was right, and he hated it. "I should leave right now. I didn't sign up for a summer of relationship complications."

"You can't leave. I know things might be a little uncomfortable with you and Paige. And I'm sorry about that. But if you leave, the kids will be in danger." He lowered his voice. "The kidnappers almost succeeded last summer. If they try again—if they're successful—it'll be the end of me. Please, Nick. I need you."

"Then come protect the kids yourself."

Don snorted. "You know I can't do that. That's field agent work."

"She looked at me like I was a pariah."

"Please. You've faced down armed assassins—you can handle one scorned ex-girlfriend. I'm not taking no for an answer here. You promised you'd help. If you back out now, I'll have to cancel the trip. The news about last year's kidnapping attempt will get out. My company will be completely ruined, which means I'll go bankrupt. You're not going to do that to me, now, are you?"

Nick clenched his jaw. "That's not fair."

"Life isn't fair. You should know that better than anyone. Call me if there are any problems." And the line went dead.

Nick stared at the phone, resentment curling in his stomach. That had been a low blow. Don didn't know much about the failed mission in Amsterdam. But he knew Devin was dead, and Nick was suspended. Don had inferred the rest.

Nick could still quit. He seriously doubted that Don would cancel the trip and send everyone home.

But what if a kid was kidnapped on the trip? Nick would never forgive himself.

And he still needed answers about Devin's death. He'd gotten nowhere in Virginia, holed up in his apartment with his computer. He'd followed every lead he could find, no matter how unlikely, and gotten nowhere. Maybe he'd make more progress here.

He opened his laptop and pulled up the encrypted document of information he'd spent the last few months tracing. It had been slow, arduous work. On the surface, all the reports of the Amsterdam mission seemed in order. But from the moment he'd gotten the call telling him to be on the next flight out of D.C., he'd felt a twinge in his gut that told him something was wrong.

Devin had died because Nick hadn't listened to that feeling.

He stared at the list of information, trying to see where the hole was. Their mission had been to intercept a shipment of blood diamonds from Africa. One of the analysts had recovered a phone conversation that hinted the kingpin of the smuggling operation would personally receive the shipment. Nick and his team had been dispatched immediately, but the raid had turned into a blood bath. The kingpin hadn't been there. The shipping containers hadn't been filled with diamonds. And Devin, along with three other agents, had died.

Nick dug the heels of his hands into his eyes, his mind aching. He'd been over this information a thousand times. It was obvious someone planted the intel, but what he hadn't figured out was how—and by whom.

It had to be an inside job. It was the only thing that made sense. But the internal investigation had turned up nothing, and his superiors were growing tired of Nick's obsession.

A group of laughing teens approached the hotel and disappeared inside, and Nick knew the first wave of students had arrived. Time to get to work. Last summer, a group of criminals targeted the tour, eager to make a quick buck. Wealthy American teenagers made kidnapping for ransom an appealing option.

Nick walked across the street and into the hotel. He stopped inside the tiny lobby, letting his eyes adjust to the dim lighting. An employee stood behind the small reception desk, talking in animated French to a young couple who held each other close. The girl had long strawberry blonde hair and stood nearly a foot shorter than her tall, lanky companion. Nick flipped through the list of student names Don had given him, wondering if these two were on the list. The elevator clanged to a stop a few feet away.

And Paige sat on a chair near the window, reading. The whisper of pages brought back memories of

Sunday afternoons spent lying underneath a shade tree, his head resting in Paige's lap as she read a book and he dozed.

A lump caught in his throat, and he swallowed it back. How was he going to deal with the Paige problem this summer?

She didn't look up, too engrossed in whatever historical novel she was doubtlessly devouring. It reminded him so much of the first time he saw her that he could almost taste the coffee.

At Devin's recommendation, he'd stopped by a new coffee shop on his way to the agency office. He should've known by the address—less than a block from the Georgetown campus—that it wouldn't be his scene. The shop had been crowded and chaotic, filled with hipsters arguing over existential issues. The noise had nearly deafened him, an assault on the senses he couldn't wait to escape.

He grabbed his cup and saw her, sitting all alone in the middle of the shop. She read a textbook as though it was the most fascinating thing in the world, completely oblivious to the chaos surrounding her. She wore no makeup, and a pencil held her copper-colored hair off her neck in some sort of twist.

He had to meet her.

Without consciously making the decision to do so, he sat at her table. She didn't look up, still reading the textbook—*An In-Depth Look at the French Revolution.*

Nick cleared his throat. She kept reading. He chuckled and took a sip of his coffee. Her posture was relaxed, her eyes glued to the page. She really hadn't noticed him. He'd never met a civilian with the ability to hyper-focus like this.

"Hello," he said. "I hope you don't mind that I sat down."

Her eyes floated up from the book, a deep sapphire blue that pulled him in. She had a dazed expression, like she was still lost in the book. "Oh," she said. "Hi."

"I had no idea the French Revolution was so engrossing."

She smiled, and it did odd things to his heart. "Did you know that Marie Antoinette never said 'Let them eat cake'? Many historians believe that a look-alike was actually planted in the market to incite a riot."

"I had no idea," Nick said. "But let me take you out to dinner this weekend. I want to hear all about it."

He still couldn't believe she'd said yes. Sometimes, he wished she hadn't. It would've been easier for both of them.

She had that same laser-focus now. Her feet were tucked beneath her, book angled toward the window for the best lighting. Nick's legs pulled him toward her, a gravitational force he couldn't fight.

She continued reading for nearly a minute before looking up. Her eyes were soft, with the bewildered look she always had when emerging from an interesting read. She shut the book, and her brow turned down in a scowl.

"Oh," she said. "It's you."

His chest ached, and he longed to reach out and brush her hair behind one ear. He could almost feel the silky strands. "Sorry. I didn't mean to startle you."

"I was startled when you showed up this morning. Now I'm just annoyed."

He swallowed. "I guess I deserve that."

She folded her arms, clutching the book to her chest. "This summer is really important to me, Nick. It's an invaluable research opportunity. I don't need any . . . distractions."

His mouth quirked up at her word choice—did she still think of him that way? She'd often accused him of making her forget her studies. But she was right—they both had a job to do, and there was no space for relationship drama.

"I'm not here to ruin your summer," he said. "I'm here to work, like you."

"Great. I'll stay out of your way, if you'll stay out of mine. I'd better go." She rose and practically ran from the room.

What had just happened?

Layla strolled into the room, pausing as Paige slipped past. Layla raised an eyebrow at Nick and slid into the seat that Paige had vacated.

"What did you do to Paige?" Layla asked. "She looked mad."

What would he have done—how would he have reacted—if their roles were reversed? If Paige had disappeared suddenly, with only a three-sentence email to explain.

His heart twisted. She deserved so much better. "Yeah, I think she is."

Layla wrinkled her nose. "What did you do?"

"What makes you think it's my fault?"

"You're the guy. It's always your fault." She smiled and took a bite of an apple. "Seriously, though. What's the deal with you two?"

How did he sum up their whirlwind relationship in a sentence? He had to say something. Layla and Tyler already knew he and Paige had dated, and the tension at breakfast had been evidence it hadn't ended well.

Best to fess up to his part in the destruction. "I broke up with her in a very ungentlemanly way."

Now Layla folded her arms, her posture defensive. "What does that mean?"

"I might have broken up with her in an email."

"Oh geez. No wonder she looks so mad. An email? Really?"

The front door opened, and three more teenagers walked inside. Nick flicked his gaze back to Layla. "I know."

Layla sighed, her eyes full of disappointment. "You seem like a nice guy, Nick. Why such a jerk move?"

"It's complicated."

"It always is. I got the sense this morning that she can be a little intense. She seemed really nice, though, until you came along. Now it all makes sense."

"I handled the situation all wrong."

Layla's gaze didn't wave. When she spoke, her tone was even and voice calm. "Okay. So how are you going to handle it now?"

Nick shrugged. "That's the question of the hour, isn't it?"

He thought about Paige for the rest of the day. He stayed close to the hotel, keeping a watchful eye on the teenagers as they arrived in small groups. He caught sight of Paige a few times, always close to a laughing Layla. Her arms were folded and shoulders hunched, but she smiled and kept up a steady conversation. He was so proud of her for accepting this job. The unfamiliar situation doubtlessly had her nerves frayed, but she was trying to push past it.

He'd missed her so much.

And now that she's here, what are you going to do about it? Nick asked himself. He had two options—keep his distance from Paige or try to make up for what he'd done.

He did another lap around the hotel, finding nothing suspicious. As he walked into the lobby, he heard Paige laugh. Her husky alto voice immediately elicited goosebumps all over his flesh. His mind flashed back to pressing her against his car door under a full moon, kissing her breathless. Her fingers running through his hair. Her waist held tightly between his hands.

And now he knew—he didn't have a choice.

Paige was here.

And he was going to win her back.

CHAPTER THREE

Paige stood in the doorway of the breakfast room, trepidation making her palms sweat as she took in the twenty teenagers filling the space. The chaperones had met that morning and decided that Layla would lead the orientation, but that didn't help Paige's nerves. The excited chatter washed over her, and she took a step back, suddenly wishing she was back in the small library housed in her father's impressive brownstone.

An arm brushed against hers. She jerked away, refusing to look at Nick. Just because they were now coworkers didn't mean they had to speak to each other any more than absolutely necessary.

A petite girl with strawberry blonde hair shrieked and jumped, knocking a bagel off the platter. The gangly boy behind her caught it with a laugh.

"Ryan Daniel West!" the girl yelled, swatting him on the shoulder. "Don't scare me like that."

One of his arms snaked around the girl's waist. "Like what?"

"You know what I'm talking about." She pushed against his shoulder, but laughed when he pulled her closer.

"I dare you to try and stay mad at me," he said. "It's impossible."

"Is that so?" She threw her arms around his neck and kissed him. Then she yanked the bagel out of his hand and pranced to a chair.

Teenagers. Why on earth had Paige thought she could do this? Her heart was somewhere in the region of her throat. If she tried to eat, no doubt her stomach would immediately rebel.

"It'll be fine," Nick whispered, his tone soft and soothing. "It's only scary until it's familiar, remember?"

Paige folded her arms, not acknowledging him. She'd struggled with mild anxiety ever since her mother's death, when Paige was only eight. Nick had somehow always known when to push her, and when to offer reassurances and let her be.

She hated that he still knew her so well. She hated that he was here.

"It's seven o'clock," Nick said, loudly enough for Layla and Tyler to hear.

Layla looked at her watch. "Time to get started, then. Are you guys ready?"

"We'll follow your lead," Tyler said.

He and Nick both looked completely at ease. So did Layla, for that matter. Paige tried to swallow the softball in her throat as she nodded her assent.

Nick's hand grasped hers in a reassuring squeeze. The movement was so brief, Paige wondered if she'd imagined it. Then she was following Layla to the front of the room on shaky legs, hoping her smile didn't look like a grimace. She wanted these kids to like her. Needed this summer to go well.

Nick ran a hand over his unshaved jaw, and her stomach gave a swoop.

"Hey, guys," Layla said, raising her voice to be heard over the din of excited students. "If we can settle down for a minute, we've got some information to go over."

The noise level slowly decreased, but two girls near the back couldn't seem to stop giggling. What was Paige going to do if she had to discipline these kids? Layla couldn't even get them to stay quiet for orientation.

Paige picked a faded fleur-de-lis on the back wall and focused on it.

"Thanks," Layla said. "Are you ready for the best summer of your life?"

Hoots and hollers filled the room as three boys cheered, half-empty plates of food in front of them.

"Excellent," Layla said, winking at the boys. "Glad at least some of you are fighting the jet lag, because we've got a city to see. I'll make this short and sweet. I'm Layla, and this is Paige, Nick, and Tyler. If you have any problems, you can always come to any one of us. We'll get to be great friends over the next few weeks."

Friends. A hysterical laugh bubbled up in Paige's throat, but she swallowed it back. She could feel Nick's eyes on her, assessing. She wished he'd stop.

"I'm sure you all went over the information packet in excruciating detail, but I'm going to go over the rules, just in case," Layla said. "Rule number one—no matter how much you love each other, members of the opposite sex aren't allowed in your room."

Paige's eyes flicked to the bagel couple, who still clung to each other. The girl's head barely came to the boy's shoulder, and his arms wrapped around her in a fierce hug. Paige caught sight of another duo near the front, their hands linked underneath the table as they exchanged secretive smiles. It was obvious there were at least a few couples in the group. Hopefully, they wouldn't be a problem.

"You're to stay with the group except during free time," Layla continued. "There will be no drinking—I don't care what the legal age is here. During free time, use the buddy system, and let a chaperone know where you'll be."

A buzzing filled Paige's ears as her heart beat rapidly in her chest. The giggling from the girls at the back grew louder. The goth boy near the front carved his initials into the wood tabletop with a fork.

This was going swimmingly.

"We're almost done," Layla said. "Girls, be quiet for just another second, okay?"

Miraculously, the noise level dropped once again. How did Layla do that? Paige was pretty sure if she said the exact same thing to this group, she'd get a completely different result.

"It'll probably take us a few days to learn everyone's names," Layla said. "Sorry in advance— we're trying our best. We don't want to be disciplinarians, but broken rules will have consequences. Everyone just be cool, okay? Then we can all have fun."

Paige glanced again at the bagel couple near the buffet table. Somehow, she doubted everyone would be "cool" for the next nineteen days.

"Well, how about we start our vacation?" Layla said.

The three boys whooped again, and the girls near the back giggled louder than ever. Paige's eyes flicked to the table of quiet students near the middle of the room, instantly feeling a kinship with them.

"Excellent," Layla said. "We've got three days to explore Brussels, before heading to Colmar, France. Today we'll visit the Manneken Pis, grab some waffles and frits, and explore downtown. Meet in the hotel lobby in twenty minutes. Bring whatever you need for the day, because we won' be coming back until dinnertime."

Chair legs scraped against the floor and kids headed for the stairs. Paige's shoulders relaxed as the room emptied, and she took a deep, steadying breath.

She'd survived her first meeting with everyone. This wouldn't be so bad.

"That went pretty well, I think," Layla said.

"You did great." Tyler offered Layla a warm smile. "You've got a way with teens."

"Maybe I should be a high school teacher." Layla laughed. "I'm heading up to the room. You coming, Paige?"

"I think I'll grab some breakfast," Paige said. Now that the meeting was over, she thought she could manage a few bites.

"I'll come with you." Tyler placed his hand lightly on Layla's back. "I've been meaning to ask you . . ." Their voices faded away as they entered the lobby.

"I'll grab something to eat, too," Nick said, his warm voice sending shivers down her spine.

Paige scowled. Her body was such a traitor. Nick wasn't worthy of warm shivers anymore. "It's a free country."

Nick raised an eyebrow and smirked. "In a manner of speaking. They still have a monarchy."

She'd almost forgotten how snarky he could be. His quick wit and playful banter had been the first thing she fell for.

Paige grabbed a croissant and a packet of Nutella, then made her way to an empty table. A newspaper sat in the middle of it, probably compliments of the hotel.

She smeared Nutella on her croissant, then pulled the paper toward her. The front page had a picture of a solitaire diamond in a gold band. She read over the headline, trying to translate it properly in her head. *Contrebande de diamants* . . . Diamond smuggling? She scanned the article, picking out phrases here and there. Terrorists. No new leads. Seemed a murder had been committed in Brussels over the weekend that authorities believed was somehow connected to the crime ring.

"What are you reading?" Nick asked.

She looked up, surprised to see him sitting beside her. How long had he been there? "Just the newspaper," she said. "I think there's a diamond smuggling ring here."

"Can I see that?" He pulled the paper toward him without asking and scanned the article.

Paige frowned, watching him read. "I didn't know you speak French."

Nick's head whipped up, his eyes meeting hers with something she couldn't quite place. Panic? "Uh, yeah," he said. "Just the basics."

"You read the article pretty fast."

"Just picking out a few words here and there." He pushed back from the table. "I'd better go pack my bag for the day."

Paige stared at Nick's retreating figure, her spine prickling with heat. He'd often taken off unexpectedly while they were dating. She'd chalked it up to his impulsive nature. Now, something felt off.

She pulled the newspaper toward her again, wondering if something had sparked Nick's abrupt departure. But there was nothing in the article that stood out. She tossed it aside. If she hadn't been able to figure out Nick while they were dating, she certainly shouldn't try and figure him out now.

Ten minutes later, Paige stood in the lobby, watching as the kids laughed together in small groups.

Nick sidled up next to her. "Hey," he said, blowing warm breath onto her neck.

She shivered, taking a step away. Stupid body. Stupid reactions she couldn't control. "Hi." She kept her voice purposefully flat.

"What are you doing?" Nick asked.

"I'm chaperoning. Making sure that no one gets left behind in the breakfast nook."

"They're teenagers, Paige, not children." His voice was soft, but the words still stung. "You don't have to watch them every second. You get to have a good time, too."

"I know that." Really, it was insulting that he thought she didn't know how to have fun. Maybe a little hurtful. They'd had some good times together before he left—at least, she had.

Nick's shoulders straightened, and he took a step back. "Okay. I'm going to see if Tyler needs anything."

"I'm not your girlfriend anymore, Nick—I don't need the play by play."

He stared at her for a moment more, then ducked outside. Paige did one last sweep of the lobby and breakfast room before leaving as well.

"Hey," Layla said. She'd pulled her hair back in a high ponytail and changed into cropped pants and a glittery T-shirt that somehow looked runway ready on her trim figure. "Is everyone out?"

"I think so." Paige tucked a strand of her copper-colored hair behind her ear self-consciously. "We should do a head count before leaving, just in case."

"Will do." Layla put her hands around her mouth, creating a funnel. "We're doing a head count, and then we'll walk to the fountain. It's only a couple of blocks."

Paige mentally recounted each teen as Tyler did the head check, and then Layla started off down the street. Paige brought up the rear, and Nick stayed uncomfortably close. Sunlight spilled over the narrow cobblestone streets as cars whizzed past. Fresh air filled her lungs as the laughter of excited teenagers warbled in the air. The kids were spread out over nearly a block, the boisterous boys and giggly girls near the front with Layla and Tyler, while the boy all in black and a few younger girls lingered near the back. Paige opened her mouth more than once to say something to the girls— to try and start up a friendly conversation—but she couldn't seem to force the words out.

Frustration built inside her, and she folded her arms, holding them close to her stomach. By the time she grew comfortable with this group of students, they'd be heading home, and she'd have to start all over again with a new group.

"Are you okay?" Nick whispered in her ear.

She jumped. "Stop sneaking up on me. It's annoying."

"Sorry. I wasn't trying to be sneaky."

"Well, you are."

He raised an eyebrow. "Again, I have to ask—are you okay?"

"Just dandy. Why do you ask?"

He motioned to the group of teens. The couple from the buffet table were slowing their pace, falling toward the end of the line. Layla's musical laugh floated back on the breeze. "I know this is stressful. I'm really proud of you for doing this."

It was the concerned boyfriend tone she'd heard so often while they were dating. His silent encouragement had been a lifeline back then. Now, it snapped like a whip.

"Stop talking like you know me," she said, her words harsh.

"I'm sorry." The words were a caress she didn't want to feel. She focused on the couple as they continued to fall back. They walked down the sidewalk with their heads pressed close together and hands in each other's back pockets. She'd felt that level of closeness with Nick once upon a time.

"Sorry for what?" she hissed.

"For everything. You have no idea how sorry. I want to make it up to you."

She stumbled on a cobblestone, pitching forward. Nick's strong hand wrapped around her arm in a moment, catching her just in time.

"Whoa there," Nick said.

She yanked her arm free and glanced at the students. The goth boy and a girl walked slowly together, the end of the line, but they were a few paces ahead and not paying attention to anything but each other.

"Stay away from me, Nick." She couldn't reconcile this kind, familiar Nick with the one who had left her. "I mean it."

"Paige—"

She quickened her pace, ignoring him. Make it up to her? What did that even mean?

Did he want to get back together?

Paige stuck close to the students for the rest of the walk, all too aware of Nick. They crossed the street, and Paige sucked in a breath, heart pounding for a different reason.

The Manneken Pis statue. They'd arrived.

It was still early—barely eight o'clock—and the crowd around the iron gates was sparse. The fountain was tucked into an alcove between two ancient buildings, stone dark with age and pollution. Flowers lined the top of the fountain as the little boy statue stood proudly. How many times had Paige seen this image in books? And now she was actually here.

In another lifetime, being here with Nick would've been a dream come true. She pushed the thought away. Nick didn't get to ruin this for her. She wouldn't let him.

Paige wrapped her hands around the iron fence, standing on tiptoes to peer over the top. She'd seen the pictures and read the facts, but the statue was still unexpectedly small, the boy standing perhaps only two feet tall. He was a foot above her eye level, relieving himself into the fountain below.

The girl with strawberry blonde hair stood a foot away from Paige, leaning into her boyfriend. "He's peeing," she said, giggling.

"Seriously, why is this fountain famous?" the boy asked.

Paige cleared her throat, and they both looked over at her. She forced away the nerves. This wasn't any different than teaching one of the undergrad courses. "There are a lot of legends surrounding the fountain. It was created around 1618, and no one is really sure why."

The girl wrinkled her nose, making the freckles stand out. "What kind of stories?"

Paige easily fell into her teacher roll, grasping onto the familiarity like a lifeline. "One of the more famous stories says that Brussels was once under siege. A little boy was a spy, and discovered a plot to destroy the city. He found the explosives and put them out by urinating. The statue was commissioned in his honor."

The girl giggled again, covering her mouth when a snort escaped. Paige smiled, feeling much more relaxed. Sometimes she snorted, too.

"I like you," the girl declared. "Do you know this much about all history, or just the fountain?"

"I know a lot about European history—I have a masters in it."

"I'm sticking with you, then," the girl said. "Ryan doesn't care about history, but I think it's fascinating. I'm Evie, by the way."

A thrill of victory shot through Paige. One of the students was introducing herself. Voluntarily. "Nice to meet you. Where are you two from?"

"New York," Ryan said. "Is that story about the statue for real?"

"No one knows," Paige said. "But the city certainly loves the statue. He has over eight hundred costumes. Looks like we've come on a day when he's not dressed."

Evie's mouth popped open. "Holy freak, that's a ton."

Paige nodded. "They display them at the museum. We'll get to see them later today."

"Wow. That's so cool!" Evie said.

Evie and Ryan moved off to talk to the group of loud boys, but Paige smiled, pleased with herself. She'd just had an entire conversation with two of her charges, and she thought it had gone pretty well.

Paige focused on the statue again and pulled out her phone to snap a picture.

Layla walked over and held out a hand. "Let me take a picture with you in it."

"Okay." Paige handed over the phone and posed as Layla snapped a few photos.

Nick watched her from a few feet away, his gaze electric. He held up one thumb, and she knew he'd seen her talking to Evie and Ryan. Known how hard it was for her, and was proud of her for doing it anyway.

She scowled and turned away.

CHAPTER FOUR

Three days, and no leads. Nick leaned against the sturdy wooden headboard of his twin bed and listened to Tyler humming in the bathroom. The wood was solid against his back, nothing like the flimsy particleboard used in hotels in the United States. Or seedy hotels in Amsterdam.

The newspaper article shouldn't have come as a shock. It hadn't revealed anything Nick didn't already know, and his friend at the agency said no new information had come in since they'd last spoke. But seeing the article—knowing the cartel was still murdering—had ignited a fire in him to find out more.

But he'd found nothing.

He closed his eyes, holding a pillow to his face in an attempt to block out the sound of running water. If he could just have a moment of clarity. If he could just think his way around this problem . . .

The internal investigation had turned up nothing. That left one of two possibilities—either the intel was faulty, or the kingpin had been tipped off and changed his plans. Either possibility seemed to indicate an inside man. But who would've had access to that information? The analysts, surely. Everyone on Nick's team. But it couldn't have been any of them. They'd lost half their men that night.

The images came then, unbidden. The dark, seedy warehouse on a canal. A glimpse of Skeeter, a druggie Nick sometimes paid for information, right before everything went south. The gunshots that had come from everywhere and nowhere all at once. Devin, falling backward into the water from a hit directly over his heart.

Nick had been ordered back, and he'd fled, knowing there was nothing more they could do for Devin. It didn't stop the guilt from eating him alive.

Devin. Paige. Was there anything he could do right?

Paige had been cold and distant the last few days, rebuffing all his attempts to speak to her. He'd watched as she interacted more and more with the students, Layla, and Tyler, loosening up and becoming the Paige he knew and loved.

Love. Two months ago, why hadn't he seen that what he felt went so deep?

Maybe he had realized it, on a subconscious level, and that's why he'd fled at the first opportunity.

His phone rang. He tossed the pillow aside and grabbed it. Don's number.

"Yeah?" Annoyance made his voice harsh. How had he not found a single lead yet?

"Hey," Don said. "How are things?"

Nick sighed. "Haven't seen anything worrisome so far."

"Good." But Don's voice didn't sound relieved. "No unsavory characters hanging around the group?"

"Not unless you count the teenagers."

"You're worried one of them might be planning a kidnapping?"

Nick rolled his eyes. It was no wonder Don hadn't lasted at the agency. "It was a joke—nothing is wrong. It's been three days of site seeing and the cold shoulder. That's it."

"So that's why you sound so grouchy," Don said, his tone cheerful for the first time. "I take it Paige isn't too happy to have you around."

"Don't sound so pleased."

"You like her, Nick. This is your second chance. Take it."

"You know it's not that easy. Things are complicated."

"That's agent life—deal with it. Keep me updated." And the line went dead.

A second chance. Nick snorted. He wanted one—more than he had realized until he saw Paige again. But she'd never give him one. Not unless he could provide an adequate explanation for their breakup. And he couldn't do that while he was still an agent. Could he?

He wasn't on an undercover mission, so he wasn't expressly forbidden from telling her anything. And he didn't need to tell her specifics—just enough to let her know why he had to leave.

It might work. The thought both thrilled and terrified him. Would Paige still have feelings for him if he admitted the truth, or had he destroyed any chance they had at happiness?

The shower shut off in the bathroom, and Nick rose, grabbing his backpack and preparing for a day of sight seeing and driving. Today they'd leave Brussels and head for Colmar, stopping along the way in Domremy and Vaucouleurs to visit some Joan of Arc sites. Honestly, Nick didn't care much where they were going. He was here for answers, not a vacation.

And okay. Maybe he was also hoping to win back Paige.

He slipped out of the room, not wanting to make small talk with Tyler. He was a nice enough guy, but Nick wasn't in the mood for anything but a croissant and yogurt. If his stomach wasn't snarling with hunger, maybe he'd be able to think clearly.

And maybe Paige would be in the breakfast room.

She was, sitting alone at the table and reading another newspaper. He winced at the reminder. He'd slipped up, letting her know he spoke French. She hadn't seemed suspicious the last few days, however—just angry.

She brushed a strand of copper-colored hair behind one ear, revealing her sharp cheekbones and slender neck. He used to love kissing her neck, right under her jaw line. It had never failed to make her sigh.

Two girls brushed past Nick, giggling. "Hi, Nick," the shorter girl said, and then they rushed to the buffet, laughing.

"Hey," Nick said.

Paige intently studied the newspaper, oblivious to everything else. Her complete lack of observational skills had made their relationship, and his many secrets, that much easier to keep. Now he wished she would question something—anything. Give him a reason to share a hint of who he really was.

She reached for her coffee cup without looking up from the paper and took a sip. Nick shook his head and headed toward the breakfast line, his stomach rumbling at the scent of freshly baked bread. He filled his plate, then looked for a seat, zeroing in on the table with the emo boy and his silent girlfriend.

"Mind if I sit here?" Nick asked the boy. He hadn't applied his eyeliner quite as dark today, and his shirt was gray instead of black.

"Sure," the kid mumbled. He angled his body more toward the girl, who lifted a spoonful of yogurt and watched it drop into her bowl.

Nick took a bite of his croissant, ignoring the couple. Sometime yesterday, he'd accepted they didn't want to be friends with the chaperones. That was fine with him. Right now, Nick didn't want to talk.

The flirtatious girls winked at him from the next table. Nick gave a half smile. He wished Paige would look up from her newspaper. Invite him to join her.

Ryan and Evie walked into the room, their muscles coiled, and faces lined with tension. Nick blinked. He had never seen them looking anything less than blissfully happy.

They headed straight for the coffee, and Evie poured them both a cup. Nick followed them with his eyes as they crossed to a table and sat down. Evie immediately leaned forward and whispered.

"I'm going to grab some fruit," Nick mumbled, rising. Emo Boy and Silent Girl didn't look up.

At the next table, Ryan scooted closer to Evie, his expression earnest. Nick dropped a scoop of fruit on his plate and walked toward them casually.

"You can't seriously be considering that," Evie hissed.

"I don't know how you can *not* consider it. What's the alternative, Evie?"

Nick paused, the hairs on the back of his neck standing up.

"It's not as bad as you make it out to be," Evie said.

"You're right—it's worse."

Evie reached for her coffee, hand shaking. "I don't want to talk about this anymore."

Ryan blew out a breath, frustration making his brow furrow. He suddenly looked much older than eighteen, as if the weight of the world was on his shoulders. "We're not done with this conversation."

"Later."

Nick's senses tingled with unease. Something was definitely off.

Evie flicked her eyes up, meeting his briefly before focusing again on her plate. Nick took a step forward, pasting on a smile. "Hey, guys. Mind if I sit?"

"Uh, sure," Ryan said.

"Thanks." Nick pulled back a chair. "Are you enjoying the trip so far?

"Absolutely," Evie said, her smile forced and overly bright. "Belgium is amazing. I can't wait to visit the Joan of Arc sites today, though."

"Me too," Nick said. His eyes flicked toward Paige. "I dated a girl who told me a lot about her."

"I bet Paige knows lots about Joan of Arc. She's the smartest person I've ever met." Evie twirled a strand of strawberry blonde hair around her finger. "Think she'll tell me some stories at the sites if I ask?"

"I'm sure she will," Nick said. "Is this your first time to Europe?"

"Yup. Ryan's been a few times, though." Evie wound the strand tighter, flicking her eyes to Ryan, then Nick, then the linen tablecloth.

"Just on business trips with my dad." Ryan didn't bother to look up from his food. "He never took me to the sites or anything. I mostly just played video games in the hotel room."

"Which is why I'm so glad we're on this trip together," Evie said. "Ryan needs a little culture."

Ryan rolled his eyes. "Right. Culture."

Okay, there was definitely something off with the couple. "Did you two get in a fight?" Nick asked. If this was some teenage drama, he'd have to refer them to Layla. He was totally out of his depth.

"Oh, you know." Evie waved a hand as though it was nothing. "Ryan isn't too excited about Joan of Arc. He's still annoyed I made him watch a documentary on the plane ride over."

Nick shifted his gaze back and forth between the couple. Why was Evie lying?

Ryan gave Evie a meaningful look. "I guess I'm just more excited for the big cities."

Evie scowled. "Hurry up and finish eating. I've still got to repack my suitcase before we leave."

Nick watched the couple leave the room, taking a bite of his fruit. Paige still sat at her table, oblivious to her surroundings.

He picked up his plate and slipped into the empty seat beside her. "Hey."

Paige glared, her eyes wandering to the newspaper. "Hey."

"Did Ryan and Evie get in a fight?"

Paige frowned, looking up at him. "I don't think so. Why?"

"I just had a weird conversation with them. I heard them arguing about something, but they wouldn't tell me what."

"Teenagers get in fights a lot. Their relationships are rocky." Paige shrugged. "I'm sure it's nothing. But I'll keep an eye on them today."

"Thank you," Nick said.

"Sure." Paige flipped a page on the paper.

Nick knew he'd been dismissed. But it felt like a victory. The beginnings of being a team once again.

CHAPTER FIVE

Paige emerged from the bus, the last one off the vehicle, and her breath caught in her throat.

Vaucouleurs. Nearly six hundred years ago, Joan of Arc had walked these grounds.

The ancient stone church was nestled at the bottom of a lush green hill, its gray exterior stained with pollution. The twenty teenagers spread out across the grounds, taking pictures and admiring the structure. It towered before them, large and impressive, especially for what had been a Catholic church for a relatively small French town in the early fifteenth century. The sweeping lines and Gothic arches evoked a reverence even the kids seemed to sense, because they were staying uncharacteristically quiet.

Evie stopped beside Paige. Her strawberry blonde hair hung over her shoulders, obscuring half of her face, but the awe with which she admired the building was unmistakable. The fact that she was without Ryan made Paige wonder if Nick was right—maybe the couple really was fighting.

"It's beautiful," Evie said.

"This is where Joan's mission to save France really began in 1428," Paige said, keeping her voice quiet.

"It's so cool you know the dates right off the top of your head. You're going to be an awesome professor."

Paige couldn't help but smile. "I've spent a lot of hours studying those dates."

"What else do you know about Vaucouleurs?" Evie stumbled over the unfamiliar French word, her pronunciation all wrong.

"Well, Joan's uncle lived in the nearby village. She stayed with him that spring, and met the military commander of the area. She tried to convince him to take her to the dauphin—you know, the heir to the French throne—so she could liberate France from her captors and restore the country to its glory."

"She was an amazing woman," Evie said, and her voice took on a wistful quality. "So strong. So sure of her purpose and her journey."

"She was." Paige gave Evie an odd look. Was there more to the fight than typical teenage drama? "Where's Ryan?"

"Oh, he's down there." Evie pointed vaguely toward one of the pathways around the backside of the church. "We sort of had a fight this morning."

"Oh?" Paige tried to keep the surprise from her voice. She hadn't expected Evie to bring it up.

"It's nothing. Ryan just likes to be dramatic." She smoothed her hair over her shoulders, and Ryan appeared from behind the church. "I'd better go to talk to him. He's probably cooled down by now."

"Good luck," Paige said.

"Thanks." Evie jogged down the small hill. Ryan met her halfway, and they slowly walked away together.

Paige met Nick's eyes from across the grass, and he strolled casually toward her.

"Did Evie say anything?" he asked, his voice low.

"Just that they're fighting. She didn't say about what."

Nick stared at the couple, lips turned down in a frown. "Something's off."

Paige pursed her lips. Evie had her arms folded. She leaned away from Ryan while he leaned toward her, his hands moving through the air in animated gestures as he talked.

Paige couldn't let Nick be right. "Couples fight—especially when they're eighteen. That isn't weird."

"Yeah, you're probably right." Nick's phone rang, and he glanced at the number. "Sorry, but I've got to take this."

The phone was already to his ear as he walked away. Paige folded her arms, forcing herself to look away. He'd tried really hard the last few days to resurrect a semblance of what they'd once had. He'd been nothing but kind, brushing off her less-than-friendly behavior as though it were nothing. It was getting harder and harder to keep up her aloof facade. The truth was that she missed Nick. She'd loved him once. Maybe she still did.

But how she could just forget what had happened and move on? He'd broken her heart and left her completely adrift. She didn't know if she could trust him again.

"Hey." Layla danced up to Paige, her footsteps light and graceful. "Was that Nick I just saw leave?"

"Yeah."

Layla frowned. "You two aren't fighting again, are you?"

"I guess not." Paige stuck her hands in her back pockets, raising her face to the sunlight. A light breeze blew through her hair, calming her soul.

"What's the deal with you two, anyway?" Layla asked.

"We dated. He broke up with me."

Layla rolled her eyes. "I know that."

"Trust me—it's really not that interesting of a story."

"Except that it is. He obviously still likes you. So why did he leave?"

That question had kept Paige up at nights. "I wish I knew."

"Oh, come on." Layla thrust out a hand, pointing to Nick's turned back. He stood underneath a tree, the phone to his ear. "He's like a scruffier Hemsworth brother. You can't tell me you don't want a piece of that."

Paige had thought of little else since Nick's arrival back in her life. He gazed at her so intensely, like she was the only woman in the world. It would be easy to fall back into their old patterns.

But having Nick back had brought all the things that had drove her crazy about him right to the forefront of her thoughts. His frequent and unexplained disappearances. The business trips that lasted for days, and somehow were always in locations with spotty cell phone service. Vague answers to direct questions.

He'd read that French article so rapidly, yet claimed to barely know the language.

"What about you?" Paige said, turning the question around. "You and Tyler seem to be getting along pretty well."

Layla smiled, a dimple popping in one cheek. "Yeah, Tyler's cool. I wouldn't say no to a summer fling, if he was interested. But I'm not looking for anything serious. Nick, on the other hand . . ." Layla shrugged delicately. "He might not deserve a chance, but *you* deserve an explanation. And he seems willing to give it."

Paige thought about that as they loaded the bus. The unknowns had eaten her alive for the past two months. Didn't she owe it to herself to at least hear him out?

She picked a seat across the aisle from Nick. He gave her a tentative smile, and she answered it with one of her own.

The bus ride to Domremy was short and oddly familiar—Paige had spent hours looking at photographs of the area. Joan of Arc's childhood home was plain in the extreme, with its two-dimensional yellow stucco exterior and slanted roof.

"So cool," Evie said as the teenagers crowded into the small building.

Paige waited outside, not wanting to fight the chaos. She heard one of the giggly girls squeal, and then the deep baritone of one of the loud boys.

"You're not going in?" Nick asked. His hands were shoved deep in his pockets, a crooked smile on his lips.

"I'll let the kids see it first." Paige rested a hand softly on the home's exterior, the sun-warmed stucco rough against her palm. Six hundred years, and still standing. Amazing.

"You had that same look on your face when we visited Mount Vernon," Nick said. "It was the first time I caught a glimpse of just how much you love history."

"I think I could stay in Europe forever." Paige pointed at a steeple, rising above the trees. "That's the church where Joan was christened as a baby. The entire course of a country changed because a little baby girl was born in this town."

The teenagers wandered out of the building, making their way toward the church. Paige glanced inside, seeing only a few of the shyer kids still there.

Nick nodded toward the building. "Go check it out. It'll be quiet now."

Paige took a step inside, then paused in the doorway. If she wanted answers, she had to start being friendly. "Aren't you coming?"

His eyebrows arched, and a soft smile played on his lips. "Yeah. Okay."

Paige placed a foot carefully on the tile floor. Joan had grown up here as a child. Probably taken her first steps in this very room. The room was open, with a fireplace along one wall and a statute of Joan in the corner. The last three girls left the room, and Paige and Nick were alone. Sunlight filtered through the heavily paned windows, illuminating the dust in the air.

"Is it everything you hoped for and more?" Nick asked.

Paige smiled. "It's pretty cool."

Nick took a step forward, leaving mere inches between them. Paige gazed up into his face, her hand aching to feel the stubble on his jaw. He reached out slowly, his fingers brushing along her cheek before tucking a strand of hair behind one ear.

"I'm glad you get to experience this," Nick said, his voice husky and green eyes dark. "I'm glad you're on this trip."

Paige took a step back, clearing her throat. Her heart beat painfully, and her stomach felt full of thumbtacks. "I should go answer questions," Paige whispered. "Layla said she doesn't know much about the history here."

Thirty minutes later, they boarded the bus, and Nick sat beside her. Paige didn't say much to him on the road to Colmar, but Nick's presence felt both reassuring and right.

They entered Colmar as twilight blanketed the town, casting it in a beautiful glow. Paige sucked in her breath as the large bus lumbered through the town. This was what she had always imagined France to look like— colorful picturesque buildings, tall and narrow, lining narrow cobblestone streets. There was even a fountain in the town square.

The bus came to a halt outside a small hotel, and Layla stood. "Free time for the rest of the evening," she announced. "Everyone better be in their room by ten p.m. Don't make me hunt you down."

The kids laughed, and the bus broke up into individual conversations as they gathered their belongings and headed off. Paige felt Nick's gaze on her, as heavy as a blanket. She knew he wanted to talk, and tonight would be the perfect opportunity. But Paige was emotionally exhausted. The progress they'd made today already felt monumental.

Nick slid out of his seat, then motioned to Paige. "After you."

Paige grabbed her backpack and made her way down the aisle, the heat from Nick's close proximity making her entire body go hot and cold. He was going to ask to talk tonight—she just knew it. She wasn't sure if she was ready.

Layla waited just outside the bus, bouncing from foot to foot. "Hey! Tyler and I thought it would be fun to all go out to dinner together." She flicked a glance between Nick and Paige. "What do you think?"

"Sounds great," Nick said. "Paige?"

She took a deep breath, then nodded. "Okay."

"Great!" Layla brushed her bangs out of her eyes. "I going to freshen up. Let's meet in the lobby in thirty minutes. The restaurant is close enough we can walk, and their bread is to die for."

Paige's mouth watered as she remembered breakfast that morning in Belgium. If it was anything like that, she was in for a treat. "You're making me hungry."

"Good." Layla winked at Nick. "I'm going to order escargot for the table, too. When in Rome . . . Or Colmar, I guess."

"I'm not eating snails," Paige muttered to Nick.

"Don't worry," he said. "I'll protect you."

She looked away, face uncomfortably warm.

In their room, Layla wasted no time strewing clothes across her bed.

"Are you changing?" Paige asked.

"I thought it'd be fun to dress up a bit." Layla held up a sparkly cocktail dress. "Too much?"

"It's pretty."

"Too much." Layla tossed it aside and picked up a glittery tank top. "Are you going to change?"

"Yeah, I guess so." Paige unzipped her suitcase and pulled out a red silk blouse. It had a deep v-neck, and ruffles around the collar. The shirt wrapped around her middle and tied on one side, making her waist look teeny. With her dark denim jeans and little makeup, she might even look pretty. Not beautiful, like Layla, but pretty.

Layla was already stripping in one corner, and Paige quickly did the same. She tied the shirt, trying not to think about the last time she'd worn it.

"Whoa, hot mama!" Layla said, letting out a wolf whistle.

Paige blushed. "Too much?"

"No way. You look gorgeous."

"Thanks." Paige played with one of the ruffles. Layla looked like a super model in her skinny jeans and silver tank top, her bangs somehow making her blue eyes pop.

"May I?" Layla pulled up half of Paige's hair without waiting for a response. "Oh yeah. You should totally pull your hair back. I have some bobby pins. Just a sec."

Paige stood still in front of the mirror while Layla worked her magic. Layla teased the top a bit, then pinned it in a half ponytail that was way more chic than anything Paige could've managed.

"Perfect," Layla said. "Nick is going to die when he sees you."

Paige grabbed a tube of lip gloss and swiped some on, just to avoid looking at Layla. "This has nothing to do with Nick."

"Sure it doesn't." Layla winked. "Let's go."

Paige's knees wobbled as she made her way down the stairs. She should've worn something a little more casual. Nick would recognize the shirt and think she was sending him some kind of message. Or maybe he wouldn't recognize the shirt—that might be even worse. She brushed her fingers along her lips, remembering how he'd kissed her after the concert. Their first kiss. She'd bought this shirt specifically for that date.

She should've stayed in her T-shirt.

Her heart skipped a beat when she saw Nick waiting in the lobby with Tyler. Nick had changed into a pair of dark denim jeans and a loose short sleeve button-up shirt, the top button left undone. The color was a deep green and exactly matched the shade of his eyes. Her mind flashed back to the dozens of dates he'd picked her up for, looking handsome and smelling like cinnamon.

Nick stopped talking. His eyes lingered on her blouse, and the green of his irises softened. His mouth turned up in a smile. For one crazy moment, she almost wrapped her arms around his neck for a kiss.

The blouse had definitely been a bad idea.

"You ladies are looking lovely this evening," Tyler said, breaking into Paige's thoughts. "Ready?"

Paige flicked her gaze over to him, noticing that he'd dressed up a bit, too. She suddenly didn't feel quite so self-conscious in her dressy blouse and fitted jeans.

"Ready," Layla agreed. She led the way outside, Tyler following close on her heels. The two were already chatting away, laughing at something that had happened on the bus ride earlier today.

"I guess we should go," Paige said, avoiding Nick's eyes. "Layla might leave us behind if we don't keep up."

"You're never lost when you're with me. I'm excellent at finding things."

Paige focused on the cobblestone. What was that even supposed to mean?

Outside, the air had grown pleasantly cool, and the sun had dipped below the rooftops. Layla and Tyler were already half a block ahead, Layla's trilling laughter floating on the breeze.

"You look amazing," Nick said. "Europe suits you."

"It's weird to finally be here," Paige said. "I've been dreaming about it for so long."

"What are you most excited for?"

She let out a happy sigh. "Everything. The castles. The Swiss Alps. Paris. What about you?"

He shrugged. "I'm just along for the ride. I've enjoyed everything on the trip so far. I'm sure I'll enjoy the rest of it, as well."

Paige deflated a little. A vague answer—she didn't know why she was surprised.

"So, where are you living now?" she prodded.

"Arlington."

She sucked in a breath, the hurt more intense than she'd anticipated. He'd only moved a thirty-minute metro ride away? "Oh. I didn't realize you were so close."

"I wasn't, when I left." His voice was as soft and gentle as the breeze. "I went abroad for a while."

"Your email said it was work related?"

"Yes."

She folded her arms, the air suddenly chilling instead of refreshing. She'd forgotten how cryptic he could be.

"Paige—"

"We're here," Layla called up ahead.

Paige quickened her pace, relieved for the interruption. He'd been the one to leave. Maybe he didn't deserve a second chance.

Nick grabbed for her hand. "Please—"

She shrugged it off. "They're waiting for us," she said. And she hurried to catch up with Layla.

CHAPTER SIX

The restaurant was small, with a thatched roof and teal flower boxes beneath each of the front windows that instantly charmed Paige.

Tyler held open the door. "After you, ladies," he said gallantly.

Layla gave a dramatic curtsy. "Thank you, kind sir," Layla said.

Even in the dark, Paige could see Tyler's face redden.

Inside, the dim lighting revealed dark wood tables dotting the room. The heady aroma of baking breads and rich pasta flooded over Paige. Oh, heavens. She inhaled deeply, letting her eyes roll back in her head.

"I'm going to gain twenty pounds this summer if I'm not careful," Paige said.

Layla laughed. "We walk enough that it mostly balances out. Told you this place was amazing."

"I'm still not eating escargot," Paige said.

"You have to try it." Layla nudged Tyler with her shoulder. "You'll try it, won't you?"

His chest puffed out, and he stood a little taller. "Sure. Sounds delicious."

"I'll try it, too," Nick said. He threw Paige a glance and rolled his eyes. "I'll even eat Paige's portion."

If he thought that was going to make her forget everything, he was dead wrong.

An older man appeared at the host stand. "*Bon soir. Une table pour quatre?*"

"*Oui,*" Layla said.

Nick's arm brushed against Paige's—just the lightest of touches, but her nerve endings felt as though they'd been lit on fire.

The mustached man grabbed four menus. "*Par ici.*"

He led them to a table in the corner of the room, and Paige flashed back to the restaurant Nick had taken her to right before the concert. It had possessed the same intimate feel as this one. Paige and Nick had lingered over their meal, heads close together as she shared tidbits from her past. That had been the night she told him about her mother's cancer and death. She'd felt safe and secure in the moment, impressed to find a man that was such a good listener. Now she wondered why he hadn't told her more about himself.

Nick stood behind a chair, holding it for Paige in invitation. She slowly sank into it, letting him push her forward.

This Nick made her heart ache with longing. She wanted a second chance with him, but was terrified to give him one.

Paige cleared her throat, focusing on Layla. "Your French is really good. Where did you study?"

"Oh, I don't know that much. I took French in high school." Layla shrugged. "What about all of you?"

"My mother was French Canadian," Paige said. Was Nick recalling the time she'd unloaded her regrets over not having a closer relationship with her mother's family? "Her parents speak almost no English. After she passed away, my father made sure I attended a private school with a strong French program. He knew my mom would've wanted that."

"That's so sweet," Layla said.

Tyler gave a sympathetic frown. "I'm sorry about your mom."

Nick's hand found Paige's underneath the table and gave it a gentle squeeze. She reflexively curled her fingers, but he'd already released her grip.

"It was a long time ago," Paige said.

"I haven't heard you speak French much," Layla said, turning to Nick. "Are you fluent?"

"I get by." Nick pulled out his phone. "Excuse me, but I'd better get this. Order the *magret de canard* for me if I'm not back by the time the waiter returns."

"You will be," Layla said cheerfully. "Dining in Europe is all about the experience. They won't take our order for at least thirty minutes."

Paige watched Nick leave the restaurant, unease prickling her stomach. Why had he never mentioned speaking French while they dated? And why was he now pretending to not be fluent, despite having read that article so rapidly?

Nick was a puzzle that was pointless to try and figure out.

"So when did you learn to speak French?" Paige asked, focusing on Tyler.

They talked about their childhoods, and Layla shared funny stories from last summer in Europe while the minutes ticked by. The waiter appeared, and they placed their orders, including Nick's.

"Where did Nick disappear to?" Layla asked. "It's been like half an hour."

Tyler shrugged. "He's always doing that. I've given up trying to figure it out."

Paige choked on the water she'd been sipping. She coughed, a loud, hacking sound that ripped through the tranquil restaurant.

"Are you okay?" Layla patted her on the back.

"Fine." Paige took another sip of water, trying to clear her throat. "Sorry. Swallowed wrong. Nick leaves a lot?"

"Yeah." Tyler's skin looked even paler than usual under the dim lighting, and freckles stood out on his cheeks. "It's not like he's gone for hours at a time, but he disappears. I figured he was calling home or something."

"Does Nick have a lot of family?" Layla asked. She and Tyler both stared at Paige with expectant expressions.

Embarrassment mixing with frustration curdled in her stomach. "He didn't talk about them much. I know his parents live in Pennsylvania, and I think he has a sister somewhere in the Midwest."

Layla raised an eyebrow. "I get it—too busy kissing to talk, huh?"

Paige blushed. "It wasn't like that."

"Sure it wasn't." Layla leaned toward Tyler, resting her chin in the palm of her hand. "Does Nick talk about Paige a lot? Give us the inside scoop. Nick is an enigma."

"Guys don't really talk about stuff like that," Tyler said.

Layla smirked. "Sure they do. What's your read on Nick?"

"He's nice." Tyler shrugged, as though that said it all.

Layla gave an exaggerated eye roll. "Men. Am I right? Oh, he's coming. Act natural."

Paige whipped her head around. Sure enough, Nick strolled back to their table.

"Sorry about that." He slipped into his chair. "I didn't expect to be gone quite so long."

"Is everything okay?" Layla asked.

Nick gave an easy smile. "Nothing to worry about. So, did you order that escargot?"

"You bet," Layla said enthusiastically. "I can't wait for you guys to try it."

Paige made a face. "Seriously, there's no way in Hades I'm eating a snail."

"Oh, come on, it's not *that* bad," Layla said. "They dip it in so much butter and garlic that it's basically like eating crab."

Right. No difference at all.

A few minutes later, the waiter set the escargot in the middle of their table. The plate had indented circles around the edges, and the snails floated in tiny pools of butter and garlic, still in their shells. Paige cringed, her face crinkling in disgust.

"Ready to try one?" Layla asked the group, her eyes alight. "They're delicious. Promise."

"Anything for you, m'lady," Tyler said. "Now, do I pull it out of the shell, or eat that, too?"

Layla laughed, leaning into Tyler. "Don't worry. I'll teach you how to eat it."

Ugh. Paige was going to be sick. Was that snail still moving? It better just be her eyes playing tricks.

A hand rested on her knee, and she jumped. Nick's fingers found hers underneath the table for the second time that night.

"Don't worry," he said. "I won't let her make you try it."

"Good," Paige said. "I don't think anyone wants to see how that would turn out."

Conversation flowed for the rest of dinner, and Paige almost forgot about Nick's disappearance. She ordered a fruit crêpe for dessert that was out of this world, and somehow found her hand in Nick's again, hidden from sight underneath the table. This time, Paige didn't pull away. His thumb softly caressed her knuckles, and she let her fingers tighten around his.

She missed Nick. A lot.

They paid for their meal, then headed outside. Darkness cast the colorful buildings in dark shadows.

"I want to show Tyler something," Layla said. "Meet you guys at the hotel?"

Paige glanced at her watch. "Head check is in thirty minutes."

"We'll be back by then." Layla tugged Tyler down the street, in the opposite way from the hotel. Tyler wrapped Layla's hand in his, and their laughter disappeared as they vanished down a side street.

"They seem to be getting along well." Nick was a silhouette in the shadows, and his husky voice made a delicious shiver run along Paige's spine.

"I think she likes him," Paige said. "And he definitely likes her."

"They'd make a cute couple."

Electricity sparked between them, and Paige longed to reach out and touch Nick.

"Are you cold?" he asked.

"No." Her nerve endings felt on fire, and the pit of worry in her stomach grew. Could her heart handle giving him a second chance?

They walked slowly toward the hotel, not bothering with the sidewalk since the streets were empty. A full moon sparkled above them, reflecting off the cobblestone. Talk about picturesque.

"You look beautiful tonight," Nick said. "I've always loved that blouse on you."

Paige tugged at the corner of her shirt. "Thank you."

"Do you remember the first time you wore it?"

"The concert," Paige said softly.

"It was a perfect date." Nick threaded his fingers through hers.

Paige's heart pounded in her chest. "I'd never had a guy plan such a thoughtful evening for me."

Nick chuckled, the sound rich and enticing in the dark. "Getting those tickets wasn't easy. But you were absolutely worth it. I wasn't about to let you down." His hand squeezed hers. "I'm sorry I ended up failing in the end."

She wouldn't get a better opening than that. A silent war waged in her mind—the need for answers battling the fear of what they'd mean.

Curiosity won. She took a deep breath, and plunged. "Why did you do it, Nick? I thought things were going well."

"They were." His Adam's apple bobbed in the dark. "It's hard to explain. I'm not sure where to begin."

Again with the vague answers. She could scream. "Fine then. Don't tell me."

A car screeched around the corner, headlights momentarily blinding Paige. She yelled, the blare of the horn making her jump. Nick yanked her out of the street. She fell against the side of a building, chest heaving. Nick was right beside her, the length of his body warm against her side. She rested her head against the brick and started to laugh.

"We almost died," she said with a gasp. "I guess it'd serve us right for walking in the middle of the street."

Nick pushed himself off the wall, his body hovering over hers. Her laugh cut off as he stared down at her, his eyes black in the darkness.

A hand reached out and slowly brushed against her cheek. "I would never let anything happen to you, Paige. You're safe with me."

"What a relief." Her voice was embarrassingly breathy.

White teeth glinted in the moonlight as he grinned. His fingers moved down her cheek and around the side of her face, until they were buried in her hair. Her scalp exploded with tingles. Nick leaned closer, and his warm breath whispered over her face, smelling like cinnamon.

"Do you remember what we did after the date?" Nick asked.

Paige couldn't tear her eyes away from his. "Yes. That was the night you first kissed me."

"It was a full moon, just like tonight."

"The parking lot was nearly empty. We'd stayed in the stadium, talking until the traffic died down."

Nick's body pressing against hers. Paige rested her hands on his shoulders, not sure whether to pull him close or push him away. Her entire body ached with longing.

"I'd spent the whole night wanting to kiss you." Nick shook his head and chuckled. "I was terrified, though."

"I kept wondering what was taking you so long."

His fingers played with the ends of her hair, and her entire body buzzed with electricity.

"I'm not making the same mistakes this time," he whispered. "I've learned my lesson."

His head lowered, and Paige arched her back, pressing closer to him. He paused, his lips millimeters from hers. Waiting.

And she knew she was lost.

She laced her fingers behind his neck and lifted on her toes. Their lips met, and then his hands were at her waist, pulling her impossibly closer. Paige ran her fingers through his hair—felt his tongue flick against her lip. With a groan, she deepened the kiss. The hard brick wall pressed into her back, but all she felt was his hands in her hair, at her back, moving to caress her face and neck. Heat blazed through her as white-hot as it had the first time they kissed.

During that first kiss, she'd known she was falling in love with Nick. And now, she knew that she'd never really stopped.

He eased away, the weight of his body lifting. Her breathing was ragged, and she longed to pull him back.

He pressed a feather-light kiss over each of her eyelids, then one on her mouth.

"We should get back," he said, his voice rough with emotion. "We'll miss room checks."

Paige rested her hands on his chest, and he pressed another soft kiss to her forehead.

"I still have questions," she said.

"I'll do my best to answer them."

Would the answers matter? He'd hurt her so much. "I'm not sure I've forgiven you."

"That's okay." He held her in a tight hug. "All I'm asking is for the chance to earn that forgiveness."

They didn't talk as they walked the two blocks to the hotel. Nick held her hand loosely, and Paige's lips buzzed from the recent attention. She could taste the cinnamon of his kiss on her lips.

She still needed answers, but for tonight, having Nick was enough.

The hotel lobby was quiet. Paige pulled her hand away from Nick's as they trudged up the stairs, and he let her go without protest. She wasn't sure she was ready to explain this—whatever *this* was—to Layla and Tyler.

In the hallway, Layla divided up the rooms. The four of them did a head check, then met in the hallway.

"All accounted for," Layla said cheerfully. Paige and the men mumbled an assent.

"I guess I should go to bed," Paige said, looking up at Nick. His eyes were like two emeralds, burning in the dark.

"We'll talk tomorrow," he said, giving her hand a squeeze. "Goodnight."

"'Night," Paige said.

As soon as their bedroom door was shut, Layla turned to Paige and squealed. "He kissed you, didn't he?"

Her cheeks burned. "Maybe."

Layla threw back her head and laughed. "Excellent. I really hope you two can work things out this summer. He's head-over-heels for you."

"What about you and Tyler?"

Layla flopped onto her bed and rolled her eyes. "Ugh. That boy moves slower than molasses in wintertime. Maybe he's just not interested."

"He's interested," Paige said. "Promise."

It took a long time for Paige to fall asleep. She kept playing the kiss over and over in her head. When she was in Nick's arms, it was easy to forget all her concerns. But in the dark, with only her own thoughts as company, they came flooding back. Had tonight really changed anything? Sure, they'd kissed. But Nick had still left two months ago. He still hadn't explained why. He was still secretive and closed off. And what had he really been doing when he left dinner tonight?

He'd scanned that diamond article in the newspaper so intensely. Something pricked at the back of her mind, but her sleep-exhausted brain couldn't pinpoint what.

Nick was such a good kisser. It made everything else seem inconsequential. She hated that.

Paige rolled over, her mind finally drifting off to sleep. Pleasant dreams of Nick wrapped her in a warm cocoon. She could almost feel his arms holding her close, his lips pressed against her.

A thud sounded outside her door, following by a quiet curse and giggling.

Paige sat up in bed, instantly awake. The voices sounded young. Like teenagers.

Layla snored softly from her bed. Paige padded across the floor. Another giggle, followed by a *shhh*.

She flung open the door. Two shocked faces stared back at her.

It was Evie and Ryan.

CHAPTER SEVEN

"What do you think you're doing? Stop right now. I said stop!"

The shrill, yet muffled, voice penetrated Nick's sleep. Paige! He was out of bed and across the room, gun in hand, before he'd fully processed the sounds.

Nick threw open the door and ran into the hallway, gun first. It took him less than three seconds to assess the situation. Paige's mouth dropped open, and Evie let out a yelp, cowering against Ryan.

Nick instantly lowered his gun, shoving it in his waistband. Crap.

"What are you doing?" Paige looked way too sexy with her tousled bed head, light cotton tank, and rumpled shorts. "Why do you have a gun?"

"I heard you screaming," Nick said. He should've peered around the doorway first, but hearing Paige's panic had erased all rational thought from his mind.

She'd seen his gun. He'd deal with that later.

Nick fixed a severe frown on Evie and Ryan. Both were fully dressed in jeans and dark shirts. Curfew breakers. Awesome.

Ryan wrapped an arm tightly around Evie, his voice lined with thinly veiled belligerence. "We were just taking a walk."

Nick crossed his arms, knowing it made his muscles bulge intimidatingly. What were the chances they'd forget about the gun? "Right—a walk. I was eighteen once. I know what's going on here."

"It was just a walk, honest," Evie said, her words tumbling over each other. "We're really sorry. I couldn't sleep, and thought a little exercise might help. I texted Ryan, so I wouldn't be out alone."

Paige ran a hand through her hair, messing up the locks even more. Nick rubbed a hand over his jaw, torn between yelling at Evie and Ryan, and dragging Paige into a dark corner to kiss her.

"How could you guys be so irresponsible?" Paige said. "The rules are there to keep you safe. Anything could've happened."

"We're sorry. We shouldn't have left." Evie's eyes were luminescent with tears. Nick barely held back a groan. Crying girls always got to him.

"Breaking curfew is grounds for being kicked off the trip and sent home early," Paige said.

Evie clutched at Paige's arm, and a tear rolled down her cheek. The overhead lights cast dark shadows over her collarbone for a moment before she shifted and her hair fell over her shoulders. "Please don't do that. I promise, it won't happen again."

Nick waved at Ryan. "Well, what do you have to say for yourself? Seems like Evie's doing all the talking."

"We're sorry," Ryan parroted, his tone surly.

Evie nodded, her bangs bouncing against her forehead. "So sorry."

Paige kept glancing at his waistband, her muscles tense. Yeah, she hadn't forgotten about the gun. No doubt they'd be discussing that very soon.

This felt like the wrong way to tell her the truth. She was already so stressed.

"I'm really disappointed in you guys," Paige said, pulling Nick back to the conversation.

"But you aren't going to send us home?" Evie asked.

With a sigh, Paige shook her head. "This is your one and only pass. Get to bed before I change my mind."

"Of course." Evie grabbed Ryan's hand and tugged. "Goodnight."

They scurried down the hallway and disappeared into their own bedrooms. Nick slowly turned to Paige, suddenly very aware that he was in his boxers, and she was in thin cotton pajamas.

Paige's sapphire eyes were dark with bewilderment. "What the heck just happened?"

Nick shrugged, deliberately misinterpreting her question. "They probably wanted some alone time."

"Not them." She pointed to his back, where the gun was held tenuously in place by the sturdy elastic of his waistband. "You ran out here like Rambo or something. Since when do you carry a gun?"

"I believe in exercising my second amendment right."

"We're in Europe—you don't have a second amendment right. Who are you, Nick? When you jumped into the hallway, I nearly had a heart attack."

He felt the gun slip in his waistband, and he reached back to adjust it. "I'm sorry. I heard you scream and acted without thinking."

"And your automatic response was to draw a loaded weapon?" She took a step back, shaking her head. "I feel like I don't even know you."

He grabbed her hand. "You do know me. I've tried to be as honest as possible."

"Then tell me what is going on here!"

His eyes flicked around the empty hallway, with the thin doors he couldn't see behind and open stairwell at one end. "Not here. I promise, I will tell you everything I can. But this isn't the time or place."

She gave a hollow laugh. "It never is. I'll let Layla know what's happening—you should tell Tyler. We'll keep a closer eye on Evie and Ryan from now on."

He stepped in front of her before she could walk away. "Don't mention the gun. Please."

Her shoulders slumped, and she nodded. "Goodnight, Nick."

"I will tell you everything."

"Sure you will." And she disappeared into her bedroom, shutting the door tightly behind her.

* * *

The next morning, the chaperones met in Nick and Tyler's room. Nick mostly let Paige tell the story. He kept waiting for her to bring up the gun, but she didn't. He would've kissed her for it, except her stony look said she was still angry.

Layla lounged on Tyler's bed, her eyes filled with outrage. "I can't believe they snuck out."

"They're kids," Tyler said. "They make stupid mistakes."

"If they make another one, I'm putting their butts on a flight home," Layla said. "Unbelievable."

"Evie really did seem sorry," Paige broke in. She'd refused to take a seat on Nick's bed, and instead stood in one corner of the room, shifting her weight from foot to foot. "I think she'll keep Ryan in line."

Nick watched Paige carefully, hoping for a hint of what today would bring. But she ignored him.

"We'll keep an eye on them," Nick said. "Hopefully they're scared enough to behave for the rest of the trip. Two weeks, and they'll be on their way home."

Layla rose from the bed with a loud sigh. "Well, we'd better get down to breakfast so I can give them the death glare."

Dark circles shadowed Paige's eyes, and she'd pulled her hair into some sort of bun with a pencil. She paused by the door, raising her eyebrow at him in a silent question.

"You go ahead," he said quietly. "I need to call Don and fill him in."

"And today you'll give me answers?" she asked.

Why, oh why, had he drawn his gun? He brushed a lock of her hair out of her face, his heart thundering in his chest. He couldn't tell her much. But would it be enough to scare her away?

"I'll tell you what I can," he said.

Paige gave a clipped nod and followed Tyler and Layla from the room.

Nick took a deep, shaky breath, then pulled out his phone and dialed Don's number.

"Hey," he said as soon as Don picked up.

"Everything still okay?" Don asked.

"Yeah, no one's tried anything. Well, no criminals, at least. Two of the kids sneaked out after curfew last night. We took care of it, and I think it was just kids being kids."

"Not surprised," Don said. "Seems like there's at least one couple every summer. Anything else of note?"

Nick thought about his phone call with Skeeter last night. He'd finally tracked him down with the help of a friend at the agency. It had taken some fast talking, but Skeeter had finally agreed to hop a train and meet Nick. Hopefully, he'd actually show.

Skeeter had been squirrelly on the phone, mostly interested in a quick buck for another high. But he'd given enough details to convince Nick his story wasn't a lie. He'd confirmed what Nick had long suspected—the intel had been a purposeful false trail. Someone in the agency had betrayed them.

"Nick?" Don prodded. "Has something else happened?"

"Nothing exciting," Nick said. "I'll keep you posted."

He checked to make sure his gun was concealed in the holster at the small of his back, then left for breakfast. His eyes immediately sought out Paige. She sat at a table with Layla and Tyler, their heads close together as they shot furtive glances in Evie and Ryan's direction. Nick wondered if the couple would mention the gun. He'd have to talk to them when there weren't so many listening ears.

Nick grabbed a plate and put a few slices of ham on it. Ryan looked surly, his arms crossed and brows pulled down in a scowl. Evie spoke rapidly, one hand resting gently on his arm.

Layla zeroed in on Nick and motioned him over. He placed a roll and a spoonful of fruit next to his ham, then sat down next to Paige.

"What did Don say?" Layla asked.

"To keep an eye on them," Nick said. "And we will. He didn't seem too concerned."

Tyler nodded in the kids' direction. "Looks like they're fighting now."

"They're mad they got caught," Paige said.

After everyone finished breakfast, they loaded the bus. Nick sat beside Paige on the drive to Titisee, Germany. But their close proximity to listening ears made discussing the previous night impossible.

Nick wrapped Paige's hand in his, weaving their fingers together. He knew that as soon as they were alone, she'd demand answers. Should he give her truths that might destroy their relationship or lies that would merely prolong the inevitable end?

He'd promised her the truth. Fear clawed at his chest as he thought of telling her everything. Could she handle it?

The bus climbed up the mountainside, weaving its way through Germany's famous Black Forest. Nick tried to quiet his mind and focus on the beauty surrounding him. Paige stayed silent, clutching his hand as though sensing that soon, everything would change.

The bus pulled into the parking lot, and Paige dropped his hand. Lush green aspens and pines covered the area in dense foliage, with thatched roofs peeking through the branches. Skeeter should be on his way to the meeting spot now. Nick checked his watch. Just over an hour until they were supposed to meet at the lake.

Layla told the kids to be back in two hours, and they quickly disappeared to explore the town.

Nick snagged Ryan's arm as he and Evie started to walk away.

"Not a word about last night," he said, giving them a glare that made grown criminals tremble in fear.

"We won't say anything," Evie said, her face pale. She glanced at his back, then swallowed hard. "We can keep a secret."

"Ryan?" Nick prodded.

"Yeah, we'll keep quiet," Ryan said, yanking his arm out of Nick's grip. "Come on, Evie."

Paige stared at Nick as the teens walked away. He carefully wound his fingers through hers. "Want to check out Titisee with me?"

"Yeah," she said, seeming as eager to postpone the inevitable conversation as he was. "There's a cuckoo clock shop here I really want to explore."

"Let's find it, then."

The warm June sun beat against their backs as they meandered up the main street of town, looking for the shop. It was easy enough to find. Beautiful hand-carved clocks cover the walls inside, ranging from a few inches tall to a couple of feet. The soft ticks of a hundred pendulums in sync filled the room.

A man with a full head of silver hair and pronounced wrinkles stood behind the counter. "*Guten morgen*," he said.

"*Guten morgen*," Nick said in return, the German words sliding effortlessly off his tongue. The vowels washed over Nick in an oddly comforting way.

"Can I help you?" the man asked, his English broken and heavily accented.

"Thank you, but we're just looking," Nick said.

The man nodded, and Nick led Paige toward the back room of the store. Their footsteps creaked against the ancient wood floors.

"Wow," Paige said, admiring the intricate spindles and delicate figurines on the various clocks. She pointed to one wall. "Look, they're all from different fairy tales."

He took a step closer, admiring the clock she stood closest to. Two tiny carved figurines stood near castle doors. One had a face like an animal, and the other wore a yellow dress.

"*Beauty and the Beast*," he said.

"It's always been my favorite Disney movie."

"Watching it with you while making cookies is one of my favorite memories."

Paige's shoulders slumped, and she sighed. "What are we doing, Nick?"

He wrapped an arm around her waist, pulling her close. "I thought we were picking up where we left off."

"*We* didn't leave off anywhere—*you* left *me*. And you still haven't given me a satisfactory explanation."

This was it, then. Paige wouldn't pretend any longer. The time for secrecy had passed. He'd tell her everything, and she'd run screaming in the opposite direction.

"I didn't want to leave," Nick said.

"You've said that."

"I had no choice."

"You've said that, too. And then last night, you pulled a gun? What was that?" She rubbed her hands up and down her arms, as though suddenly chilled.

He glanced at the open doorway. Another tourist could walk inside the shop at any moment. "We should go outside."

Her jaw clenched, and her eyes burned with determination. "I'm not going anywhere until I get answers."

"I don't know how much I can tell you." He thought of all the secrets he'd kept and lies he'd told during their time together. An agent's life was never easy, and adding relationships only complicated things.

But he couldn't lose Paige again.

"You aren't an accountant, are you?" Her blue eyes were sad, and a little scared.

Forty minutes until he needed to meet with Skeeter. "No."

She put a hand to her forehead. "I'm such an idiot. All the phone calls you had to take, the dates you cut short or canceled. I thought you had a weirdly demanding job for an accountant. I thought you were flighty and impulsive, which was annoying but part of your charm. But all that time—you weren't really staying late at work or helping a friend move or any of those other excuses you gave me."

He took one of her hands in both of his, slowly massaging the tense muscles. "I didn't want to lie to you, but I had no choice."

"Who are you, Nick?"

He scanned the room, but they were still alone. The tick-tock of the pendulums was loud enough to drown out any sound. He took a step closer, then lowered his voice and plunged ahead. "I'm a government spy."

CHAPTER EIGHT

"Are you serious?" she said, her voice hoarse. Surely she'd heard him wrong.

A government spy. Well, at least there was a reasonable explanation for him carrying a gun.

Paige stared at Nick, feeling as though the floor had just fallen out from underneath her. Their four-month relationship rearranged itself in her mind as puzzle pieces that had always seemed off fit into place, revealing a very different picture.

Nick ran a hand through his hair, his muscles coiled with agitation. "We really shouldn't be talking about this here."

She folded her arms, anger replacing her disbelief. "You promised me answers. Start talking."

He sighed, his eyes darting about the room. When he spoke, his voice was so low she had to lean closer to hear. "I was working on an important undercover mission while we dated and couldn't risk anyone finding out the truth. I wanted to tell you so many times."

Sure he did. Her nails dug into the soft flesh of her arms. "For what agency?"

"It's better if you don't know. I doubt you've heard of it, anyway."

"Is that why you left?"

"Yes." His eyes were dark, the emerald green deeper than she'd ever seen it. "I had a mission overseas, and I didn't know when I'd be able to contact you again. I regretted breaking things off—especially the way I did—as soon as I had a second to stop and think. But I knew that if I did it in person, you'd ask too many questions that I couldn't answer. At the time, it seemed like the easiest way."

She took a step back, needing to put some distance between them. Her legs shook, and the room suddenly felt ten degrees warmer. "Wait. Is that why you're here now? Are you on another mission?"

He paused, and the silence that stretched between them felt like the beginnings of another lie. A volcano brewed in Paige's chest as the clocks ticked ominously. Nick stared at her, his eyes saying things Paige was terrified to understand.

"Don had some security concerns," Nick said. "Nothing major, but I'm here to help him out."

"And that's all?" Paige pressed.

"I'm not here on the agency's behalf."

A screech filled the air, and Paige jumped. Hundreds of cuckoo clocks chirped, little birds jumping from the houses as they counted off the hour. Ten o'clock.

Nick reached toward her, but Paige took a step back. The birds disappeared inside their houses. The tick tick tick of their pendulums seemed louder than ever now, a time bomb doomed to explode.

"Please, Paige. It's not a good idea to talk here. Let's go to the lake."

She was going to be sick. Every conversation and moment spent with Nick now contained the possibility of a lie. "Was finding a girlfriend part of your cover mission? Was I just a pawn in your little game?"

"Absolutely not. Relationships are . . ." Nick shook his head fiercely, eyes luminescent with pain.

"Are what?" Paige demanded, making her voice acidic.

"Are dangerous!" Nick exploded. "I never should've asked you out. There's a reason men in my line of work stay single. But I couldn't help myself, and I fell in love with you. I'm still in love with you."

The words washed over her like an ice bath, and her entire body tingled with a delicious sort of pain. "Wh-what?"

"I love you, Paige. I thought about you every single day we were apart."

The words were right, but the situation was all wrong. He was supposed to have said these things after a romantic evening stroll past the Washington Monument, not after disappearing for two months. She glanced at the clocks on the walls, refusing to meet his gaze. "I don't even know who you are. Our entire relationship was a lie."

He grabbed her arms, forcing her to stand still. To look at him. "This" —he motioned back and forth between them— "isn't a lie. When we kiss, it isn't a lie. My feelings for you are real. Yes, I had to sometimes lie for my job. But I always told you the truth when I could."

"You should have tried harder to tell me the truth. I would've understood why you had to leave." She could still remember the disbelief that had washed over her when reading his email. The anger that had consumed her as she peered into the windows of his empty apartment. For two months, she'd agonized over what she'd done wrong. She'd grieved for a relationship that had been consumed by secrets.

"I know," he said. "But the lies are over. I won't leave like that again."

"You can't seriously expect me to believe that."

He ran a hand through his hair, his expression pained. "Let's take a walk. I'll tell you as much as I can."

She knew what he really meant—there were still secrets he had to keep. Helplessness welled within her, and tears threatened. She never should've come to Europe. She wished Nick had stayed hidden. "There's nothing left to say."

He let out a frustrated growl. "Didn't you hear me? I said I love you. *Love* you, Paige. I-want-to-spend-my-life-with-you-and-grow-old-together love. If I thought you didn't feel the same, I'd walk away right now. But I think you love me, too. And if I have to fight for us, I will. If I have to spend a lifetime convincing you to trust me again, I'll do it. Just let me in."

Love. Was it possible for a heart to explode with happiness while shriveling with despair?

A bell jingled from the front room, and the rough consonance of German floated through the store.

Nick's posture stiffened, and he moved so his back was to the wall. His eyes scanned the room, lingering on the doorway. "We should go."

Paige gave a sharp nod. "Fine. The lake then." She was mad enough to push him into it, if given the chance.

Outside, she squinted against the bright sunlight. A government spy. Did he run around at night, assassinating whomever the president deemed a threat? Did he skulk around seedy bars collecting information? Flit from woman to woman, like some James Bond wannabe?

He'd looked so confident with that gun in his hand. So ready to shoot. Like he'd killed before and would do it again without hesitation.

She stomped toward the lake. Nick easily kept pace beside her, his tall frame looming over her petite one. The smell of pine and fish mixed with the humidity, making her stomach turn. Water lapped angrily against the shore. Sunlight bounced dizzily off the surface.

"So you're a government spy," she said flatly. "You couldn't tell me when we were actually in a relationship, but now that we're merely coworkers who sometimes make out in the dark, you suddenly think it's fine to blurt out that little detail."

"I'm not on an official mission now. The rules are . . . looser."

Anger flared again. "Right. I'm sure the agency was perfectly happy to grant you vacation time so you can play bodyguard to a bunch of high schoolers vacationing around Europe. Spies do that sort of thing all the time."

"My last mission didn't end well." His shoulders were hunched, hands deep in his pockets. "I'm on leave while things are cleared up."

He was so dang cryptic. It took a lot of effort to unclench her jaw enough so she could speak. "Were you fired?"

"More like suspended."

"Okay. What happened on that mission?"

Nick took a step back and folded his arms. "It's classified. But we lost a lot of good men that day. When I returned to the States, I was in no condition to talk to anyone."

Her heart was suddenly in her throat as she imagined gun-wielding thugs pointing their weapons toward Nick. As she imagined his life in danger. His gun raised in defense. "Did you kill someone?"

His jaw clenched. "No. Someone killed my partner."

She sucked in a breath.

"He was my best friend, and I couldn't save him." Nick's face twisted with pain.

"I'm so sorry." All the anger drained out of her body, leaving a hollow emptiness in its place. She knew how it felt to watch someone you loved die. As young as she'd been when her mother passed away, the memories of watching the cancer decay her mom into a shell still haunted Paige.

"As soon as I left, I knew I'd made a mistake. But Devin . . . well, it's complicated." The sunlight reflected off the water, casting shadows on his face. "I want a life with you."

Paige put a hand to her forehead, nausea making the world spin. Talk about a flood of information she'd never dreamed of receiving. Her mind flashed back to a dozen details that finally added up—the way Nick would sometimes get a phone call, then abruptly leave. How sometimes, after a day at the 'office,' he'd have this faraway look in his eyes and not seem altogether present in whatever conversation she was attempting to engage him in. How sometimes he'd kiss her with a desperation that had confused her to no end once he disappeared.

"Say something," he begged.

"I don't know what to say." Her heart demanded she believe him, but her head argued it was a very bad idea.

"Say you'll give me another chance."

"I . . . I don't know." Nick had taken her life and flipped it upside down, leaving her bleeding and unsure of the future. "How do I know you won't disappear again?"

"I might—that's the reality of the job. But it won't be like last time. You'll know I'm leaving. I'll always tell you as much as I can. We can stay in contact as much as the mission allows, and I'll always come back."

The image of him holding a gun took hold of her heart and squeezed.

He was a government agent. He chased criminals for a living.

He played dangerous games, and he played for keeps.

"Unless you die," she whispered.

"I'll do my best to keep myself safe."

The fact he didn't promise to stay alive wasn't lost on Paige. She put a hand to her forehead, not sure what to think. What to feel.

He took a step closer, resting his hands on her arms. This time, she didn't pull away.

"I'm going to fight for you," he said. "I'll prove that you can trust me. What we have is more real than anything I've ever felt. I can't throw that away."

Paige stared up into his green eyes. "I never said it wasn't real."

He ran his hand up her shoulder, sliding it around her neck.

Maybe they could make this work. Maybe he really did want her.

"You missed me just as much as I missed you," he said, his lips brushing against her ear.

She clung to his arms to keep herself from collapsing. *Missed* seemed like such an inadequate word for what she'd felt while he was gone.

His lips brushed across her cheek, then trailed kisses along her jawline. She dug her fingernails into his biceps, her mind swirling with confusion.

And then his lips were on hers, hard and insistent. One hand pressed against her back while the other tangled in her hair. She'd missed this. She'd missed *him*.

But he'd lied to her. He'd left her bruised and broken. It was unlikely anything would change as long as he was a government agent.

She tore her lips from his, shoving him back. "No."

"Paige—"

"No!" The scream rang out across the water, and a nearby flock of birds took for the trees. She held up one shaking hand. "You lied to me for months. Now you drop a truth bomb on me, and think a few kisses will make it all better? I was a mess when you left."

"I'm so sorry." The lines in his face filled with agony. "If I could change—"

"But you can't," she cut in. "And this time, *I'm* the one who's leaving."

He grabbed her hand, but she shook it off. She needed time to figure this out. Time to think, away from his intoxicating lips.

"I'm not giving up," he called to her retreating back.

"Good," she said, so quietly she knew he wouldn't hear. Impossibly, she hoped that there was a way to fix this. To fix *them*.

But she didn't turn around, and kept on walking away.

CHAPTER NINE

Nick watched Paige walk away, the sunlight making her copper-colored hair glow. His chest tightened as a scream fought for release. He'd finally told her everything, and she had walked away. The worst part was that he knew he deserved it.

Tears pricked at his eyes, but he blinked them back. Agents didn't cry. They also didn't give up. He had three months left of chaperoning. That would have to be enough time to win Paige back.

He also had three months to figure out what had happened in Amsterdam. Talk about crappy timing. But he was used to working around messy schedules.

Paige disappeared around a building, taking a piece of his heart with her. Maybe he should've run after her and forced her to let him explain. But what more could he say? She had to come to terms with this on her own.

Nick sighed, forcing the confrontation with Paige out of his mind. Right now, he needed to switch into agent mode. He only had fifteen minutes to get to the other side of the lake. Skeeter wasn't likely to wait.

Nick walked along the dirt path at a leisurely pace, conscious of tourists who might take notice of him. The trees grew thicker the farther he moved from town. Nick broke into a light jog, confident he was now hidden from prying eyes.

Their designated meeting spot was only one-point-six miles away—a third of the way around the lake—but the trail ended after only a mile. Nick would have to blaze his way through the aspens and pines soon enough, which made it ideal for maintaining anonymity.

Thick foliage muffled the sounds of boaters on the lake. Right now, Paige was probably perusing one of the many tourist-traps lining the main street of Titisee. He wondered if Layla had found her and realized she was upset. Would Paige tell Layla everything?

No. Angry as she was, he knew that Paige would keep his secret.

Nick came to the small clearing that he'd told Skeeter about and stopped, checking his watch. Eight minutes until the appointed meeting time. Hopefully Skeeter would have real information today. He was one of Nick's more unreliable informants, but he was the only one who might actually know something about that night.

A bird chirped in a nearby tree, and Nick thought he saw a silver fox tail disappear into the forest's depths. He leaned against a tree trunk, letting his posture relax while his eyes scanned for signs of danger. He could have his gun out of its holster and firing in seconds if necessary.

He never knew what to expect from Skeeter.

Ten minutes passed, then fifteen. Had Skeeter changed his mind? Not gotten on the train?

Had he told someone dangerous—someone like the kingpin—that Nick was waiting for him?

A branch cracked from behind. Nick whirled, grabbing for his gun. He should've left as soon as Skeeter didn't show.

A man in a ratty gray T-shirt with long, greasy black hair stepped into the clearing. His shorts hung halfway down his butt, plaid boxers exposed.

He let out an expletive in Dutch, grabbing at the waistband of his shorts as they sunk lower with the movement.

"What are you doing?" Skeeter asked, glaring. "Put that away."

"You're late," Nick said, not lowering the gun.

"I got held up at my last . . . appointment."

Nick knew what that meant—he'd met up with a drug dealer for something to get him by. Nick scanned the tree line, ears perked for any noise while he searched for something out of place.

"I'm alone," Skeeter said. "Don't you trust me?"

Not for a second. Nick lowered his gun. "Can't be too careful."

Skeeter ran a hand over his eyes. Nick could see the tell-tale tremble, even from several feet away. Time for another hit.

"You said you'd pay," Skeeter said. "I need five hundred euro in cash."

"We agreed on three hundred."

"I'm not talking for anything less than four."

"Okay then. Have a nice day." Nick headed toward the trees, back the way he'd come.

"Wait!"

Nick paused. Worked every time.

"Fine. Three hundred."

Nick turned around, smiling. "Sure, three hundred—*if* your information is good. I don't have time for your lies."

"Okay, okay." Skeeter held up a shaking hand. He'd gotten a few new tattoos since Nick had seen him last. "What do you need to know?"

A bunny darted across the clearing, racing for the bushes. Skeeter jumped and let out a curse.

Nick didn't flinch. He eyed Skeeter, keeping his expression fierce. "What were you doing at the warehouse that night?"

One of Skeeter's tattooed hands skittered across his jaw. "Don't make me say it."

Nick just folded his arms.

"I was meeting with my dealer," Skeeter said. "Happy? I didn't have enough cash, though, and he blew me off."

"You expect me to believe that you just happened to meet with your dealer, right outside a warehouse where my partner died?"

Skeeter shrugged. "He said he was doing double duty."

The ring of truth made Nick straighten. "What do you mean?"

"He was watching the place for the crime boss. I don't know his name—no one does. But he runs that side of town."

Nick's blood ran cold. "Why was he watching the warehouse?"

"What do you think I am, an idiot? I didn't ask questions, and he didn't volunteer nothing. But you guys showed up not long after. You figure it out."

Nick stared at Skeeter, letting these new details drop into place. The whole thing had been a setup from the beginning, just like Nick had suspected. But why hadn't they killed every agent there? Half the team had escaped.

It didn't make sense.

"I want the name of your dealer," Nick said.

Skeeter let out a wounded grunt. "You trying to get me killed?"

"The name, or no money."

"If I give you his name, he won't sell to me anymore. I'll have to buy the crap from coffee houses, like everyone else."

Nick looked at his watch, making the motion exaggerated. "It was great talking to you, Skeeter. Enjoy the soft drugs."

"Okay, okay." Skeeter's left eye wouldn't stop twitching. "He goes by Racer. I don't know his real name."

Racer. The name didn't sound familiar, but Nick's team had been focused on diamond smuggling, not illegal drugs.

Nick pulled three hundred-euro notes out of his pocket. Skeeter grabbed for the cash, counting it eagerly. He shoved it in a pocket, the glee on his face unmistakable.

"Don't spend it all in one place," Nick said and jogged into the trees.

Maybe he'd been going about this all wrong. What if it wasn't someone on the diamond smuggling team that had leaked the intel, but someone working with the drug side of things? His head pounded with each footfall through the dense forest. Something still didn't fit.

He needed to find out more about this Racer character.

Nick burst through the tree line and onto the pathway surrounding the lake. He slowed his pace, not wanting to draw attention. The docks were fuller than they had been during his confrontation with Paige. The sun neared the top of the sky, and he knew without looking at his watch that soon the bus would be loading.

Deal with Paige. Fix his relationship. Find out who the leak was. Avenge Devin's death. And he only had three months in which to accomplish everything.

The honking of car horns and bustle of shoppers on the main street of Titisee drowned out the sound of tourists laughing as they rowed into the middle of the lake. Nick wandered down the main road, peeking his head into shops and hoping to see Paige. He tried to place himself in her situation—imagine how he'd react if their roles were reversed. A lump formed in his throat. Learning she had a life he knew nothing about would be devastating.

He caught a glimpse of the flirtatious girls outside a restaurant, giant cones of different flavored eis in their hands. Maybe if he bought Paige one, she'd forgive him. He smirked as he imagined chasing her down, the chocolate ice cream a puddle thanks to the unforgiving sun.

Then again, it certainly couldn't hurt.

Evie and Ryan stepped out of a Christmas shop, their tense postures immediately attracting Nick's attention. Evie's arms were folded, her strawberry blonde hair falling over her face. Ryan said something, moving his hands wildly as he spoke.

Evie pointed to another shop, and Ryan held open the door. They both disappeared inside.

Interesting. It seemed like sneaking out hadn't helped the fighting.

Nick crossed the street and opened the shop door. An impressive collection of hand-carved wooden tankards splayed out on the tables, but Evie and Ryan were nowhere to be seen.

Nick nodded at the bored shopkeeper behind the counter, a round woman in her thirties with tired eyes. He caught a glimpse of movement behind a tall shelf near the back of the room.

"It's not as bad as you make it out to be," Evie's high voice said.

"You're right—it's way worse." Ryan's words were harsh.

"College starts in three months. That's not too long to wait it out."

What were they waiting out? Nick picked up a tankard, pretending to examine the castle carved into it.

"You know they'll convince you to stay home somehow," Ryan said. "He's not going to let you move into the dorms."

"He'll hurt my mom if I don't."

So there was abuse going on at Evie's home. Nick strained to hear better, his stomach coiled with anger.

There was a rustle of fabric, and Nick caught a glimpse of Ryan through the racks, his arms wrapped around Evie.

"I can't stand the thought of you going back there after this trip," Ryan said. "Let's talk to my dad. He can help."

"No," she said. Nick could hear the tears in Evie's voice. "It's killing me to imagine what he's doing to my mom while I'm gone. He was furious she let me go on this trip in the first place. It's so much money."

"You didn't pay for it—I did," Ryan said. "Well, my dad did."

Nick raised an eyebrow. He hadn't realized Ryan came from such a wealthy family.

"Same difference to him" Evie's voice dropped. Nick couldn't hear what she mumbled next.

"I love you, Evie," Ryan said, and there was a desperation in his voice that Nick recognized only too well. "I can't let him keep hurting you."

"Let's not talk about it anymore. Come on, help me pick a postcard to send to my mom. Something that'll let her know I'm okay, but that won't make Steve beat her to a bloody pulp."

Nick's hand fisted reflexively. He shifted, and the butt of his gun pressed against the small of his back.

Evie and Ryan moved around the shelf. Nick slid behind it, holding his breath and praying they hadn't seen him. They spoke to the person at the cash register, paying for something—a postcard, Nick assumed.

What was he supposed to do with this information? Evie was eighteen—a legal adult, free to live her own life. But if someone was hurting her, she deserved an out. He chewed on his lip. This was police work, not agent work—he was completely out of his depth.

Maybe Paige would know what to do.

Nick eased out of the building, keeping to the shadows as he trailed Evie and Ryan back to the bus.

Paige waited on the hot pavement, watching the teens board. She smiled at Evie and Ryan, then climbed onto the bus after them.

Nick crossed the parking lot, keeping his walk casual. He made his way down the aisle, relieved to see that the seat next to Paige was empty.

Layla leaned against the back of a chair while she and Paige talked.

"Hey, Nick," Layla said. "Did you have fun?"

"Sure." Nick slid around Layla and slipped into the seat next to Paige.

"What are you doing?" Paige hissed.

Layla looked back and forth between them, grinning. "No, it's fine. I wanted to sit with Tyler anyway."

Tyler walked from the back of the bus, as though summoned. "Everyone's here."

"Great," Layla said. "We'll talk more later, Paige."

Layla and Tyler made their way up the aisle, claiming empty seats near the front. The bus lurched forward as the excited chatter of the kids bounced off the ceiling.

"I thought it was pretty clear I needed space," Paige said through clenched teeth.

"I need to talk to you."

She put a hand to her head, rubbing at her brow. "I appreciate the explanation, Nick. Really, I do. But this" —she moved a hand back and forth between them— "is too much."

A knife twisted in Nick's chest, but he shrugged it off. "That's not what I want to talk about right now. I'm worried about Evie and Ryan."

Paige's posture instantly straightened, her blue eyes bright and alert. "Did you catch them trying to sneak off again?"

He almost wished he had. "No, but I overhead another interesting conversation. Something's up with Evie. I think there might be domestic violence at home. What do you know about her?"

"Oh no." Paige's lips turned down in a frown. "I don't know much about her, to be honest. We mostly talk about history, and she doesn't mention home. I know Ryan comes from a fairly well-off family, though. All I know is that his dad's a businessman, whatever that means."

Nick pursed his lips. That fit—Ryan had said he paid for Evie's trip.

"Do you really think Evie is being hurt?" Paige asked. Her face was pale.

Nick thought of the shadow he'd seen on Evie's collarbone the night the couple tried to sneak out. He should've recognized it immediately for what it really was—a bruise. She'd worn long pants and jackets the entire trip.

"Yeah, I do."

"We should confront her. Maybe we can help."

Nick was already shaking his head. "That almost never works. There's always someone the victim is trying to protect. Let's just keep an eye on them and stay close."

Paige's eyes clouded. "I guess so."

Nick nodded and sank back against the headrest.

"I'm not ready to deal with the other stuff yet," Paige said.

"Okay."

"I'm only going to let you sit by me if you agree not to bring it up."

"Okay," Nick repeated. He was smart enough to know not to push her on this. Not yet.

"Fine then." Paige turned, angling her body to face the window. She peered out intently, watching the forest fly past as they drove toward Interlaken.

Nick closed his eyes. How had he gotten himself into this mess? And how was he going to fix it?

CHAPTER TEN

The past few days in Switzerland had lasted an eternity. Paige kept a close eye on Evie and Ryan, while simultaneously working hard to avoid Nick.

A government agent. How was she supposed to move forward with that information?

The clang of cowbells rang over the mountain as Paige strolled down the path, reveling in her solitude. Vibrant green grasses waved gently in the breeze, and the city of Interlaken spread out far below her, the homes now the size of a doll's. She desperately needed to recharge after spending so much time with noisy teenagers, and this seemed the perfect place to do it.

Nick still wanted her—he'd made that abundantly clear. And her heart ached for him. But he was a different person to her, now. She wasn't cut out to be the girlfriend of a spy.

Paige stepped off the path and lay down on the cool grass. She closed her eyes, inhaling deeply. In. Out.

In. Out. She focused on relaxing each muscle in her body and listened to the sound of each breath. The sun beat down on her. A blade of grass tickled her arm. Birds chirped quietly in a nearby tree. She forced her mind to go blank and let herself feel.

"Beautiful, isn't it?"

The voice was quiet and familiar, and Paige didn't startle at the sound. Somehow, she'd known he'd find her here. She squinted against the sunlight, and Nick peered down at her.

"What are you doing?" he asked.

Paige sighed and sat up. "I was enjoying the peace and quiet."

"That's definitely in short supply these days. I'm going to miss the kids when they leave, but it's hard to think when they're around."

Paige couldn't agree more. To her surprise, she'd grown close to quite a few of them—including Evie—and would miss them when they went home in another week. But their constant energy drained her.

Nick sank onto the grass beside her. "There's nothing like this in D.C."

Paige laughed. "What, you're not a fan of the concrete jungle?"

"I much prefer this. I mean, look at it." He thrust out an arm.

In the distance, a tram hung suspended in the air as it made its way up the mountain. Paige had dug her nails into her palms the entire ride. The tram had swayed in the breeze, making her stomach clench in fear. She'd cringed as the goth kid and giggly girls pressed their hands against the glass, exclaiming over the beauty of the world below. She'd met Nick's eyes across the tram and wished she could bury her face against his chest until they were safely on the ground.

"This kind of reminds me of the nature preserve I took you to," Nick said. "Not the mountains, but the wildflowers. The fields were purple with them. Remember?"

Paige ducked her head, her cheeks hot. She remembered, all right. "Yeah. That trip was just fantastic."

A low rumble burst out of Nick. He held a hand to his mouth, shoulders shaking. "I had no idea you hated nature so much."

"I grew up in classrooms, not camping in the Wild West. We can't all be Rambo."

Nick's shoulders continued to shake. "I thought you were going to have a heart attack when that moth landed on your shirt."

Paige had screamed, running around the clearing until Nick had grabbed her and insisted the moth was gone. "It was big enough to be a bat."

"That tiny thing? It was probably more scared than you were."

"It ended up being a pretty good night." Paige couldn't keep the wistfulness from her voice. Nick had taken her back to the city. They'd watched the sunset from the steps of the Lincoln Memorial, locked in each other's embrace.

He'd gotten a phone call just as the sun sank below the horizon, shattering the magical moment. His mom had a flat tire and needed help. At the time, she'd gone gooey over what an obviously devoted son he was. Now she wondered if he'd really left on some sort of spy mission.

A fly buzzed around her head. Paige flinched, batting it away.

Nick chuckled. He reached out with one hand, catching the fly mid-air. He tossed its body into the grass.

"How often did you lie to me while we were dating?" she asked.

Nick frowned, resting his arms on his legs. "Only when necessary. I always told the truth when I could. I hated keeping things from you."

"If we'd kept dating, would you have eventually told me the truth?"

Nick clasped his hands together, shoulders hunched. "The rules were different then. I was on an undercover mission—I couldn't tell anyone who I was without permission from command. Even now, I'm walking a gray line."

Tears pricked at her eyes, and she looked away. "That's a no, then."

"I didn't say that." He gently grasped her chin, forcing her gaze back to his. "But I spend most of my time undercover. Command wouldn't have granted permission unless we were engaged."

Paige couldn't look him in the eye—*engaged*. They'd only been dating four months when he left.

"Did you think about us getting married?" she asked, her stomach tied in knots. She certainly had, and all too often for a relationship that was still in the beginning stages.

"Yes. I worried a lot about how you'd react to the truth. Life with a spy isn't easy. When the mission came up, I wondered if it was fate's way of telling me to let you move on."

"And now?" she whispered.

He brushed a hand along her jaw, making her skin tingle. "Now, I want you—forever."

Tears filled her eyes, and she blinked them back, looking away. She wanted so badly to take that promise and run off into the sunset with it.

But reality would come crashing down around her soon enough. It was better to deal with the facts before her heart was any more involved.

"You're doing more than chaperoning kids in Europe this summer," she said. It wasn't a question.

"Don has security concerns. Last summer, some kids were almost kidnapped."

Paige blinked, her breath catching. "What?"

"I think it was just an unfortunate coincidence. I haven't noticed anything suspicious, other than Evie and Ryan."

Paige shook her head, forcing herself to focus. "That's not what I'm talking about. You get phone calls and disappear. You were gone for almost forty minutes at dinner in Colmar. Tyler spent an hour looking for you in Titisee, but it was like you'd vanished after we talked. He says sometimes he wakes up in the middle of the night, and your bed is empty. That's more than protecting a group of high schoolers from a kidnapping that seems unlikely to ever happen."

He stared at her, his green eyes hooded and dark. Paige wrapped her arms around her knees, trying to stop the trembles that shook her body.

"Don't lie to me," she said, her voice tight. "If you really love me—if you want even a prayer of us having a future together—you'll tell me the truth."

Her heart pounded in her chest. The muscles in his arms were coiled with tension, his back hunched and face toward the ground.

He was going to stand up and walk away. She took a deep breath, determined not to cry until he was gone. If he couldn't be honest, she didn't want him.

It was better this way. Life with Nick would be a constant challenge—filled with secrets. It would be completely, utterly different from the quiet life she'd always imagined. History professors and government spies didn't end up together. They were too different.

"There's a lot that's classified," Nick said. "But yes—I'm here for another reason, too."

Her head shot up, and she stared at Nick, hope blossoming in her chest. Was he actually going to trust her with the truth?

"It's not official agency business. In fact, if my bosses found out, they'd turn my suspension into a dismissal before I could blink. Helping Don wasn't the only reason I came to Europe. Finding you again was simply a bonus."

He was going to tell her. She picked at a blade of grass, tying it into a knot.

"My last mission went bad," he said.

"The one where your partner died?"

"Yes. Something about the mission struck me as wrong from the very beginning. When we got there . . ." He sighed, running a hand through his hair. "Well, it was an ambush. Men were falling right and left. The rest of us barely escaped."

Paige put a hand to her mouth, envisioning Nick dodging bullets. A sick pit formed in her stomach. He could've died.

But he hadn't. And now he was letting her in—giving her a glimpse of who he really was. He was being honest.

It felt like the start of a new chapter in their relationship. Was it possible that a spy and history professor could have a happy ending?

She could deal with almost anything, as long as he told her the truth.

"The internal investigation turned up nothing," Nick said. "But I know in my gut that someone at the agency betrayed us. I'm not going to stop until I find out who it is."

"And you'll find that information here?" Paige asked. He was actively looking for danger, and it made her nauseous with fear. If they picked up where they'd left off, this would be her life.

"It's the only lead I have," Nick said.

"That's why you were suspended."

"Yes." His mouth quirked up in a smile. "My superiors don't look kindly on agents who question their investigations. But I've got a friend helping me out. It's better if I don't tell you who."

"Be careful, Nick." She placed a hand on his arm, desperation clawing at her insides.

"I always am."

She wanted to beg him to stop searching—ask him to give up his career and build a nice, quiet life with her.

But asking him to leave would be asking him to become someone different. He'd turn into a Nick she didn't know. And she really wanted to know this Nick—the real Nick—better.

She could be brave for him.

He placed a hand behind her head, a question in his eyes.

She gave the smallest of nods.

He brushed his lips gently against hers, the touch feather-light. She clung to him, wrapping her arms around his neck and pulling him closer.

No one could guess what tomorrow would bring. But she had this moment—this day. Right now, she had Nick.

He kissed her one last time, then pulled away, putting some distance between them. Her heart pounded, and her breathing rushed out in a whoosh of air.

She wanted him, baggage and all.

"For the first time in a long time, I feel like it's going to be okay," Nick said.

She closed her eyes, letting the words run through her. Then she said two words in response. "Me, too."

CHAPTER ELEVEN

The next day, they left Interlaken and headed back to France. For three days—his best since their breakup—Nick explored castles with Paige. They seemed to have reached a tentative truce, and he found himself hoping that by the end of summer, she could begin to trust him again.

As for Nick, there were two people he definitely didn't trust—Evie and Ryan. He hadn't caught them breaking curfew again. But they were constantly having whispered conversations together, and the way the hair stood up on the back of Nick's neck told him that something was up. Paige agreed, but there wasn't much they could do other than keep an eye out.

"They're talking again," Paige said, eying the couple. Evie and Ryan sat near the front of the bus, their heads close together as they whispered.

"They haven't interacted with anyone else this entire trip," Nick said. They'd be to Paris in a half hour, tops—the last leg of this tour—and he was no closer to figuring out what was up with Evie and Ryan, or finding the double agent.

"We can't let them go home without saying something," Paige said. "It's irresponsible. What if Evie is in serious danger?"

Nick had worried about the same thing. He'd spent some time digging into Evie's past but hadn't discovered anything particularly shocking. Her mother had remarried a few years ago, and the police had visited the house numerous times. Her step-father had a long rap sheet of petty crimes, and her mother had a history of unstable relationships. Evie was caught in the middle of a destructive cycle.

"We'll talk to her on the last day, if nothing has changed by then," Nick said. The bus went over a bump, and Paige bounced into him, leaving a trail of heat in her wake. "But she's an adult—we can't force her into anything. If she wants to go home, we have to let her."

"She's barely eighteen." Paige's eyes burned with fury. "She's probably terrified. Her automatic response will be to deny anything's wrong and go back to her mom."

"And we'll give her options," Nick said. "Ryan will be on our side. Maybe, between the three of us, we can come up with a plan. But for now, let's watch and see."

Paige nodded, biting her lip. He could tell she wasn't sure he'd made the right call. He wasn't sure, either. The pang in his gut made him uncertain.

"It'll be weird to see all these sites with a new set of kids," Paige said.

Nick enveloped her hand in his. "I'm glad we get a chance to do it all again. This time, I want to see everything with you."

She blushed, the tips of her ears glowing red. "I'd like that. There's a lot of Europe left to visit."

He knew what she was hinting at. Yesterday, Paige had casually mentioned she was taking the Chunnel to London as soon as all the teens were on a plane. They had five days off before the next tour started, and Layla and Tyler were going with Paige to England. Nick had a feeling she wouldn't complain if he invited himself along.

But Nick had other plans. He was headed to Amsterdam, where he'd track down Racer. Hopefully, he could put an end to this investigation once and for all. And once he did, he'd plan a future with Paige.

Maybe even one that included a career change.

"There it is," Paige said, her face pressed to the glass.

"What?" Nick asked. And then he saw it—the Eiffel Tower. It rose toward the sky, lights glittering in the dusky sky.

"Amazing." Paige glanced at Nick, grinning. "I've literally dreamed of this moment my entire life. I bet the view from the top is spectacular."

"Tomorrow," Nick said, kissing her cheek. "Is that what you're most excited to see?"

"Yes. No." She laughed, and her eyes drifted back to the Eiffel Tower. "Don't make me choose."

"It is pretty magnificent." It had taken his breath away the first time he came to Paris, too. But he'd never made it to the top. That was a first he'd share with Paige.

"I can't believe they were going to tear it down after the World Fair in 1899. Everyone thought it was a monstrosity. Did you know it attracts more visitors than any other paid tourist attraction in the world?"

He smiled, tracing her lips with his finger. He loved the way her eyes lit up when she spoke of history. "I didn't know that."

"You don't seem as impressed by the Eiffel Tower as I'd expect you to be."

"I'm impressed. Promise."

Her eyes narrowed. "You've been here before, haven't you?"

"A few times, yeah."

"Right. I should've realized."

He rubbed a thumb along the back of her hand, wishing he was free to tell her everything. "I'm sorry."

The words were inadequate to express everything he wished he could say.

"Did you do much site seeing?" Paige asked.

He guessed that depended on her definition. Crowds made for a great place to drop off a package or pass along a message without drawing a lot of attention. "I've been to a lot of the more popular tourist landmarks. But I was busy at the time, and not looking at it as a tourist."

She nodded, her eyes grave with understanding.

"I've never been to the top of the Eiffel Tower," he said. "My first time will be with you."

Her smile returned, but the creases around her eyes and tightly pressed lips spoke of the effort it took. "I think I'm most excited for the Eiffel Tower, and then the museums. Versailles is in a category all its own. Did you know the palace has seven hundred rooms? As many as three thousand people would live there at a time."

The passion in her voice fascinated him. Everything about Paige pulled him in. He'd felt the wall between them ever since his return, but he was slowly breaking it down. "What museums are you looking forward to the most?"

"Probably the Louvre. I know, I know—it's a little cliché. But I've been dying to see Napoleon's Apartments."

That surprised him. "You're not most excited about the Mona Lisa?"

"I guess. But there are lots of historical artifacts in the Louvre that aren't just oil on canvas."

"So the Mona Lisa isn't historically significant?" he said, teasing now.

Paige slapped him on the arm. "That's not what I said. But the Mona Lisa is for the tourists who want to pretend they marveled at the secrets held within the Louvre. There's so much more to that building—to the history inside—than one piece of art."

Nick laughed, wrapping an arm around her shoulders and pulling her against him. He kissed the crown of her head. "I love you."

She snuggled against him but didn't say it back. That was okay though. He could wait until she was ready.

"Oh my gosh," one of the girls squealed from the back of the bus. "Guys, the Eiffel Tower!"

The bus exploded in noise as teens looked up from their phones to find the famous structure. Paige rolled her eyes, and Nick laughed.

Traffic was congested, and the bus inched toward their hotel at a crawl. Finally, they piled into the spacious hotel lobby, which housed two couches and chairs surrounding a fireplace.

"Ritzy," Paige said, looking around the room. "We can almost all fit in here without getting claustrophobic."

"Things are definitely not as roomy in Europe," Nick said.

"It's part of its charm," Paige said.

Ryan, his face lined with stress, pushed his way toward the reception desk, where Layla handed out room keys. Nick scanned the room and found Evie near the back of the group, biting her nails.

He hoped she'd accept help. Ryan's family seemed respectable and influential. Maybe they'd be willing to help. The couple seemed to really love each other.

"Head check at ten," Layla said, voice raised over the chatter of excited teens. "Stick with your travel buddy, and if you're paying more than two euro for one of those stupid Eiffel Tower keychains, you're overpaying. Have fun!"

"I want one of those stupid Eiffel Tower keychains," Paige said.

Nick laughed. "I'll buy you one in every color."

"They come in different colors?"

He leaned down, brushing a soft kiss across her lips. "Yes. I can't wait to show you the city."

Layla pushed her way through the kids, Tyler right behind her. Nick had noticed an increasingly stupid look on Tyler's face as the weeks progressed, and had a hunch that he and Layla were more into each other than they let on. Nick wondered if he had the same expression on his face when he looked at Paige.

"Okay, break it up, you two," Layla said, grinning. "We're going shopping."

Paige raised an eyebrow. "Like to the mall?"

"No, we'll go to the Forum des Halles tomorrow. I'm talking about tourist shopping. The Latin Quarter is the best place to buy souvenirs, and it's only a few blocks away. Want to come?"

Paige glanced at Nick, and he swallowed back a rush of emotion. He loved that she looked to him before confirming her plans, like they were a couple again.

"Shopping sounds great," Nick said. "My sister told me I'd better buy a snow globe for her, or I'd get my butt kicked."

Paige's blue eyes dimmed, like a shutter had pulled closed. "You have a sister?"

Nick stared at her, pain shooting through his heart. He'd never talked much about his family because it was easier to keep his cover story straight without details about them interfering. "Yeah. Just the one."

Layla looked back and forth between them. "After four months of dating, you don't even know that much? Geez, come up for air occasionally." She bumped her hip against Paige's. "Can't say I'm surprised he's that good a kisser."

"He looks pretty taken to me," Tyler said, his voice tight.

Layla laughed, linking her arm through Tyler's. "I'm not planning on fighting Paige for him. Should we drop our stuff off in the rooms, then meet back here in five minutes?"

"Sounds like a plan," Paige said.

The elevator actually fit all four of them at once, and soared to the fourth floor without creaking. Nick and Tyler said goodbye to the girls and let themselves into their room. Nick could hear the shrill laughter of the giggly girls in the room next to theirs. That would make sleeping tonight a treat.

"Why don't you just tell her you like her?" Nick asked, dropping his suitcase at the foot of the bed nearest the door.

Tyler flinched, the tips of his ears glowing red. "What are you talking about?"

"Oh, come on—I've got eyes."

Tyler ducked his head, focusing intently on the zipper of his backpack. "She's way out of my league."

"Oh, I don't know about that. I think she likes you, too."

"Layla's nice to everyone."

Nick clapped Tyler on the back. "Take a risk. It might just pay off."

"You and Paige seem to have worked things out."

"We're trying to."

Tyler slipped into a jacket and checked his reflection in the mirror. "She's a really nice girl. I'm happy for you guys. I hope you can get through your issues and stay together after the summer's over."

"Me, too, man. Me, too." Nick held up his phone. "I've got to make a quick call. Meet you in the lobby?"

"Sure," Tyler said.

Nick grabbed his own jacket, then slipped into the hallway, dialing Don.

"Hello," Don said cheerfully, his high voice screeching through the line.

"We made it to Paris," Nick said. "Still no signs of anything suspicious from the outside."

"Keep watching," Don said. "I'm not taking any chances."

"I've got to be honest, Don—I think you're being paranoid." Nick glanced around the hallway, then lowered his voice. "The only suspicious people I've seen are Evie and Ryan."

"They're just kids. I don't think you have anything to worry about."

"Maybe not, but I'm keeping an eye on them just the same. Paige and I want to talk to Evie before she goes home. We're worried about the situation."

"Can't hurt," Don said. "Stick close to them and keep me posted."

"Will do," Nick said, and he hung up.

Nick took a seat in the lobby, and Tyler arrived two minutes later. The girls were, of course, five minutes late. But the wait was worth it. Paige had done something to her hair, so that it hung around her shoulders in loose curls that had him aching to kiss her. She'd changed from her capris into pants, and the jeans hugged her legs and hips in a way that had his mouth going dry.

"Beautiful," he said and kissed her.

She looked down, smiling shyly. "Thanks."

"Stop kissing," Layla said. "There will be plenty of time for that when you're back in the States. Tonight, we're shopping. Let's go." She grabbed Tyler's hand and towed him toward the door, although it looked like he was following pretty willingly.

Paige shook her head, a small laugh escaping. "Layla is one of a kind."

"Yes she is. Tyler is smitten."

"Did he say something to you?"

Nick pulled her forward. "If we don't keep up, Layla is going to leave us behind."

City lights flickered from windows as they followed Layla and Tyler down the sidewalk, staying a few feet back.

"Does Tyler really like her?" Paige whispered, leaning close.

"He definitely has a crush."

"Layla does, too. For someone who's so open and outgoing, she's surprisingly hard to read. You don't have any spy mind tricks to use on her, do you?"

"Uh, no." Nick's heart swelled. It was the first time she'd ever referred to his profession so casually.

"Dang. I was hoping you did."

That made him laugh.

They spent the next two hours buying souvenirs in the Latin Quarter. Paige bought a picture frame for herself and a paperweight for her dad, and Nick bought an Eiffel Tower for his sister and key chain for Paige. The evening was practically perfect. For the first time, Nick felt like there was a good chance their relationship might actually make it.

After head check, he kissed Paige goodnight and went to bed. Nick slept soundly, his hand resting lightly on the gun hidden underneath his pillow. With Devin gone, the agency didn't hold the appeal it once had for him. Maybe—once he found those responsible for Devin's death—he'd turn in his badge and do private security or something. For Paige, he could give up his career.

A knock on the door ripped Nick from his dreams. He grabbed the gun and jumped the three feet to the door, peering through the peephole. Paige stood on the other side, her eyes wide and panicked.

Nick shoved the gun in his boxers and threw the door open. She was still in her pajamas, mascara smudged underneath her eyes and hair wild from sleep. It had to be close to five a.m.

The pained look in her eyes terrified him.

"What's wrong?" he demanded.

Paige collapsed against his bare chest, her shoulders shaking. "We should've known. Should've stopped them."

Panic clutched at Nick, and he gently pushed Paige back, forcing her to look at him. "Tell me what happened."

"Evie and Ryan are gone."

CHAPTER TWELVE

The words burned as Paige spoke them. She folded her arms against the chill that had suddenly invaded the hallway, wanting Nick to welcome her back into his embrace. His eyes were dark and unreadable, but any traces of sleepiness had disappeared.

"Gone?" he said. His bare chest gleamed under the poor hotel lighting.

Paige closed her eyes, the panic freshly washing over her. "Yes. Evie's roommate knocked on my door about ten minutes ago. She woke up and couldn't find Evie. I checked Ryan's room, and he's gone, too. No one's seen them since about ten-thirty." She struggled to control the shrill note entering her voice. They could've been gone for more than six hours. They could be anywhere. Had they even left on their own?

She shuddered, shivers wracking her body. What if they'd been kidnapped?

"Calm down," Nick said, rubbing his hands up and down her chilled arms. "Maybe they ran out for a bite to eat or something."

"At five o'clock in the morning? No. It's something else. I can feel it."

"Let's not jump to conclusions. Have you checked the hotel?"

"Layla's doing that right now."

"Okay. Give me two minutes to get dressed and wake up Tyler."

She caught his arm, stopping him from going inside his room. "You don't think they were kidnapped, do you?"

Nick's back was rigid, his muscles taut, but his eyes were clear and honest. "No. But I wouldn't put it past them to run away. They've been acting suspicious since the moment this trip began. Get dressed. If Layla doesn't find them in the hotel, we'll have to search the city."

Paige nodded, racing back to her room. She threw on the first pair of clothes her hands touched and ran a toothbrush over her teeth.

The door creaked open, and Layla walked in, her face pale.

"Nothing," Layla said. "This is bad. What are we going to do?"

Paige massaged her forehead, feeling the dull pinpricks of pain that signaled a headache. "Nick and I are going to search the city."

"There are like two and a half million people here. How are you going to find two teenagers?" Layla sank onto her bed, letting out a strangled laugh.

"Nick's resourceful." Paige pulled out the elastic holding up her hair and quickly brushed it back into a ponytail.

"I could kill those two. They've been all over each other this whole trip. I bet they're in some hotel, enjoying a little alone time."

Paige's stomach turned over as she remembered the conversations Nick had overheard between them. She really hoped that was all this turned out to be. She checked the battery on her phone, then shoved it in her pocket. "I have my cell. See if you can get anything else out of the roommates, and let me know if you find anything."

"I will." Layla's eyes were ringed with sleep and worry. "Good luck."

"Thanks." Paige shut the door and ran straight into Nick.

He steadied her with his hands. "Ready?"

"Ready," Paige said. "Where do we start?"

"Right here in the Latin Quarter. Hopefully, someone saw them leave and can tell us which direction to head."

They ignored the elevator and jogged down the stairs, Paige struggling to keep up with Nick's longer stride. A quick stop at the front desk confirmed the shift had changed, and the employees hadn't seen Ryan or Evie.

As Nick and Paige stepped outside, the cool air brushed her skin. The city was oddly quiet, the sounds of revving engines muted in the early morning. The cobblestone street was still shrouded in darkness, the barest hint of light barely visible on the horizon.

"Do you have any good pictures of them on your phone?" Nick asked.

"I know I have one of Evie. We took one together at the Chateau de Villandry."

"I think I have a group shot with Ryan in it. It'll have to be good enough. Look." Nick pointed to a shop half a block away. A man carefully arranged apples in a fruit stand underneath wide window awnings. "Maybe he saw them leave."

Paige scrolled through her pictures as they strode toward the man. She paused, staring at the photo. Evie and Ryan stared back at her, their faces glowing with excitement as they posed in Claude Monet's gardens. Paige had completely forgotten that she snapped the picture. Had that really only been yesterday?

"Bonjour," Nick said as they approached the man. His back was rounded with age, and his eyes were cloudy with cataracts.

"Bonjour," the man said.

Paige held out the phone, speaking rapidly in French. "We're looking for these kids. They're with our tour group and have disappeared. Have you seen them?"

The man took the phone from her hands, squinting at the small screen. "I don't think so," he said, handing the phone back. "Sorry."

Paige's stomach dropped, and she shoved the phone back in her pocket. "Okay. Thank you."

"It's okay," Nick said as they walked away. "We'll find them."

They spoke to four more shopkeepers who didn't recognize the photos. Paige's hope dimmed with each dead end. She blinked back tears as they turned down yet another street.

"This is hopeless," she said.

Nick wrapped his arm around her in a quick side-hug. "Don't give up. We've only talked to five people."

"How many do you typically talk to?"

"Depends. Usually, I have more to go on than two teenagers who've been acting suspicious." He pointed to a crêpe cart, where a woman mixed batter. "But they didn't vanish into thin air. Someone has to have seen them."

Paige took a deep breath, then nodded. They quickly crossed the street and approached the woman at the crêpe cart. A hairnet covered her hair, and the sleeves of her jacket were pushed up nearly to her elbows.

"Bonjour," Paige said, holding out her phone. "We're looking for these two kids. Have you seen them?"

The woman wiped her hand on an apron, then pulled glasses off her head and placed them on her nose. She carefully examined the photo for ten seconds. "Oui."

Paige's heart pounded, and she put the phone back in her pocket. "You have?"

"Where were they headed?" Nick broke in.

The woman pointed toward the metro station across the street. "I saw them almost an hour ago. They were in quite a hurry."

Nick bolted toward the station, his long stride carrying him across the street.

"Thank you!" Paige said to the woman and raced after him.

Nick slowed his pace, allowing Paige to catch up.

"Did their roommates have any idea where they might have gone?" Nick asked.

"None," Paige said, remembering the panic in Angie's voice. "It's not like they've really hung out with anyone but each other since we got here."

"Do they know what time they left?"

"Sometime between ten-thirty and five a.m. That's a pretty big window."

"I think it's safe to say it was closer to five," Nick said. "That woman saw them an hour ago, and they wouldn't stick around the neighborhood for long. Everything shuts down at night, and the metros haven't been running long."

"Where would they go?"

Nick chewed on his lip, jogging down the metro steps. It was after six a.m. now. Men with briefcases and women in heels walked briskly down the steps, ready for a day at the office.

"Ryan's trying to protect Evie," Nick said. "Those conversations I overheard . . . I think he was trying to talk her into running away with him. I assumed he meant when they got back to the States. Guess I was wrong."

Paige's entire body trembled with adrenaline, and panic coated her every thought. "They can't stay in Europe. They don't have work permits. Visas. There are laws and regulations in place."

"I doubt they've thought that far ahead."

"Of course they haven't—they're kids." The muggy, stale air of the station hit Paige full force. She grabbed her metro pass, but Nick pulled her to the side, leaning against a graffitied concrete wall.

"They're legal adults," Nick said. "But we'll find them and help if we can. I should've listened to you and brought up our concerns earlier."

"I didn't have to take your advice," Paige said, hearing the misery in her voice. "This is as much my fault as it is yours. What are they thinking?"

"They're thinking the trip is about to end and she doesn't want to go back to being abused." Nick pointed to the ticket counter. "Layla didn't hand out the metro passes, right? That means they had to buy one. Maybe he remembers something helpful."

"Again, I ask—where would they go?"

Nick shrugged. "My guess? One of the train stations. I doubt they'll stick around Paris for long."

Paige's heart thumped in her chest. She unzipped her jacket, feeling suddenly overheated. "We have to tell their parents. Alert Mr. Dawson."

"We will. Soon." He grasped her hand, tugging her toward the ticket counter.

"Train tickets cost money. How much can they have access to?"

"Ryan probably has a credit card with a limit higher than either of us can qualify for."

Ideas whirled in Paige's brain, until one finally flickered to life. "That's good. A credit card can be traced."

He grinned, eyebrows raised in surprise. "Yeah. Very good, Paige."

"I've watched TV."

"The kids probably have, too. I bet they made a large cash withdrawal and bolted. That's what I would do in their situation."

"But you're a trained spy."

Nick stiffened, and Paige quickly looked around, realizing she'd spoken too loudly.

They waited in line while a mother pushing a baby stroller spoke to the attendant behind the glass window. Nick stepped forward as soon as she was done.

"Bonjour," Nick said.

Nick nodded at Paige, and she fumbled for her phone. She pressed it against the glass, and the attendant glanced at it with a bored expression.

"Have you seen either of these kids this morning?" Nick asked. He'd dropped all pretense of not knowing French, but Paige couldn't worry about that lie right now.

The attendant folded his arms. He was young, perhaps college aged, with a thin goatee and thick-framed glasses. "Who wants to know?"

"They're part of our tour group," Paige said. "They went missing this morning. We think they might need our help."

The man's eyes were hard and unforgiving. "Sounds to me like they don't want to be found."

Nick tensed. "He knows something," he said in English, his voice low so only she could hear.

"Please," Paige said in French. "We're really worried about them."

"They seemed fine when I saw them," the attendant said.

"So you have seen them," Nick said. "Where were they headed?"

The man shook his head, smiling widely.

"They probably paid him to keep quiet," Nick said, again speaking in English. He pulled out his wallet and grabbed a few hundred euro. He snapped it in front of the glass. "Is this enough to break your silence?"

The man's eyes narrowed. He looked around, then motioned for Nick to slide it through the coin slot. Paige blinked, and the money was gone.

"They bought a day pass for the metro," the attendant said. "They asked what the quickest route to Amsterdam was, and I told them which line would take them to the Gare du Nord. That's all I know."

"Amsterdam?" Paige clutched at her throat, horror flooding through her.

"That's all I know," the attendant repeated. "Now beat it. You're holding up the line."

Paige stepped away, her entire body going numb. "What are we going to do? Those stupid kids. They don't even speak Dutch! What are they thinking?" London would've made so much more sense.

Nick's face was deadly pale, his green eyes distant and muscles rigid.

Alarm bells went off in Paige's head, and she grabbed his arm. "Nick?"

"Let's head back to the hotel." His voice was strained.

Panic blossomed freshly, and her heart raced until it hurt. She'd never seen him look so worried. "What's wrong?"

"I think it's time to call Don."

CHAPTER THIRTEEN

Amsterdam. Nick barely registered the Parisians streaming past as he and Paige fought against the current and climbed out of the bowels of the metro station.

It had to be a coincidence. There was no way the kids were connected to his mission gone wrong. They would've known how to get to Amsterdam without asking for directions.

"I think we can safely rule out kidnapping," Paige said. Her shoulder brushed against his as they crossed the street. "Seems like they left willingly."

"It definitely wasn't a kidnapping." His mind struggled to put together the puzzle pieces, to solve this mystery and make the pit in his stomach disappear.

"What are you going to tell Mr. Dawson?"

Don would lose it. Nick rubbed a hand over his jaw, the short hair prickling against his palm. Their friendship was probably going to be strained for a while.

"The truth," Nick said.

Paige let out a groan. "He's going to fire us. Evie and Ryan will end up as some unsolved mystery on one of those Sunday night specials."

"No one is getting fired." Not if he could help it, anyway. "And I promise you, we'll find Evie and Ryan. But this is Don's company, and his reputation is on the line. We need to find out how he wants us to proceed."

"How would you proceed, if this was your mission?"

Nick suddenly missed Devin with a fierceness that took his breath away. They'd worked together on cases seamlessly, almost able to read each other's minds after so long together. It had made them an effective team. "I'd make sure it wasn't a false lead, then be on the next train to Amsterdam."

They dodged a street artist setting up his easel. The sun rose over the tops of the buildings, bathing the city in a warm glow. Paige's eyes were wide, her hair frizzing out of its ponytail.

"Do you really think it's a false lead?" she asked.

"Maybe. I'm hoping we can find out more at the Gare du Nord."

"This is a nightmare." Her voice was high and thin, tension threading through every syllable.

Nick wrapped an arm around her shoulder, and she leaned into him. She'd held up like a champion so far, and he was beyond proud of her. "We're going to figure this out. I'm a trained agent, remember? We've got this."

Paige nodded, her head bobbing against his shoulder as they walked. "So we'll call Don and go from there."

"Yes. Everything's going to be fine." But he couldn't shake the feeling that he was missing something critical, just out of sight.

Inside the hotel, bleary-eyed teenagers ate in the breakfast room, ready for another day of sightseeing. Nick peeked inside. Layla and Tyler sat only a few feet away at a table near the door, heads close together as they spoke in low voices.

"Psst," Nick whispered.

Tyler looked up, his eyes meeting Nick's. Nick took a step back and leaned against the wall so none of the teens would see him.

Tyler and Layla appeared moments later, their faces drawn and eyes filled with worry.

Layla looked back and forth between Nick and Paige. "You didn't find them."

"No," Paige said. She quickly related what they'd learned at the metro station. The feeling of wrongness tugged at Nick with every word. What was Ryan and Evie's plan—to disappear in Amsterdam, assume new identities, and live out their lives? Ryan had to know his father would never be okay with that. The man had enough money and resources to mount a large-scale search for his missing son.

Maybe it was a false lead, and the kids were actually headed somewhere else. But that didn't make sense, either. It wouldn't slow down the private investigators for long.

Why not wait until they were back in the States, and run away then? Why not just tell Ryan's father what was going on and use the West family money to protect Evie?

"I can't believe they ran away," Layla said. "I tried talking more to their roommates. Neither of them heard anything during the night. Either Evie and Ryan were very quiet, or their roommates sleep like the dead."

"Probably the latter," Nick said. "They're all tired after two weeks of traveling."

"Do you really think they're on their way to Amsterdam?" Tyler asked. The freckles stood out starkly against his pale cheeks.

"I don't know what to think," Nick said. "Paige and I are going to call Don—Mr. Dawson. We'll see where he wants us to go from here."

Layla's shoulders slumped. "I can't believe this is happening. What do we tell the rest of the kids? They're going to notice that Evie and Ryan are gone."

"Tell them as little as possible," Nick said. *Need to know*. It was a phrase that had been drilled into his head for years.

"Yeah, okay," Layla said.

"Keep us posted," Tyler added.

Nick nodded, and he and Paige trudged up the stairs. He opened the door to his hotel room and motioned her inside. Why Amsterdam? He wracked his brain for a connection to the city, but he couldn't remember either Evie or Ryan ever bringing it up. Surely Italy or Spain, or even England, held more appeal for two teenagers.

Then again, Amsterdam did have some pretty loose recreational drug and alcohol laws. Maybe the kids were looking forward to endless nights of partying with daddy's money. But in order to access that money, they'd need a credit card or ATM. And those would both leave a trail.

Paige perched on the edge of Nick's bed, her arms wrapped tightly around her torso. She looked ill, her skin sallow and lips nearly white as she pressed them together.

"I'll put it on speaker phone," Nick said. He dialed Don's number, taking slow, even breaths. He could do this.

The phone rang and rang and rang. Nick fought the urge to pace, not wanting to let Paige know just how nervous he was. He thought maybe it would go to voice mail, but eventually, someone picked up.

"Hey, Nick." Don's high-pitched voice sounded tinny through the phone's speakers. "Sorry, I was in the other room. What's going on?"

"You're on speaker phone," Nick said. "I've got Paige with me. You might want to sit down for this one."

"What happened?" Don asked. Nick could already hear the panic thrumming through his voice.

Paige twirled a lock of hair around one finger, her eyes dark and frightened.

"Two of the kids have disappeared," Nick said, forcing himself to be direct. He clutched the phone until his joints ached. "We think they've run away."

Silence filled the room.

"Don?" Nick said.

"Who?" Don asked, his voice tight.

"Evie and Ryan."

A whoosh of air crackled across the line, and Don swore. "Tell me everything."

Nick filled Don in on their search. Paige's finger grew white as she twisted and untwisted the strand of hair. Nick sank onto the bed next to her, and she leaned against his side.

"Amsterdam," Don said when Nick had finished.

"We can't be sure, but yeah, I think so. I texted a friend who's going to keep an eye on the credit cards for me. I should have more information on that soon. I think it's time to call their parents."

"No," Don said. "It'll be better if we tell them after the kids have been found."

"Don—" Nick began.

"You can find them, can't you?" Don cut in.

"Yes." Nick made sure his tone held all the confidence he felt. He'd tracked down trained spies all across the world. Finding two teenagers would be easy. Boring, almost.

Except something felt wrong. What wasn't he seeing?

"Then you've got to go to Amsterdam," Don said. "Take Paige with you. Sometimes people are more willing to give information to a pretty face."

Paige nodded eagerly.

"No," Nick said, his voice rough. "I'm trained for this sort of thing. Paige isn't."

"I want to help," Paige said, hands on her hips. "You aren't leaving me behind this time."

The words hit like a punch to the gut, and from the fire in her eyes, Nick knew she was serious. But he couldn't take Paige to Amsterdam. His chest tightened as he heard the gunshots. Saw Devin's body thrown into the water.

"I feel just as much responsibility for them as you do," Paige said. She stood, her slight frame barely taller than his sitting.

"You have to think about the other eighteen kids that are still here," Nick said. "It isn't fair to Layla and Tyler to abandon them."

"Layla and Tyler will understand," Paige said, placing a trembling hand on her hip. She looked scared enough to pass out, but her lips were set in a determined line. "It's three days of sightseeing in the city, and then an airport drop-off. I think they can handle it."

"Don't be ridiculous," Nick said, fear making his voice harsh. He couldn't ignore the dread curdling in his stomach.

"It's settled then." Don's tone was final. "You and Paige will go to Amsterdam and find the kids, and Layla and Tyler will stay in Paris and finish out the tour."

"Nothing is settled," Nick said hotly. He squeezed his eyes shut, trying to block out the image of Devin's face as he fell. He'd been almost gleeful, his expression frozen in a final moment of triumph. Devin had been so confident they'd get to arrest the kingpin. Then one bullet had changed everything.

"You're both going," Don said. "I won't take no for an answer. Keep me updated. You've got twenty-four hours, then I'll have to call the parents. Don't make me do that, Nick." And the phone went dead.

Paige placed her hands on either side of Nick's face, forcing him to look at her.

"We can do this," she said. "I can help."

Nick closed his eyes, defeated. Refusing Paige would shatter the tentative trust they'd built. Besides, Don was the boss—he got to make this call.

"Okay," Nick said. "Pack your bag. I guess we're going to Amsterdam."

CHAPTER FOURTEEN

The walls of the hotel room felt like they were closing in around her. Paige took a shaky breath, rubbing her chest to try and ease the tightening. Nick still sat on the bed, his expression filled with something that looked uncomfortably like defeat. Did he think they wouldn't find Evie and Ryan?

"So we're going to Amsterdam," Paige said, her voice cracking in the silence. "We need to let Layla and Tyler know what's happening."

Nick tapped a finger against his leg, eyes growing unfocused. "It's too easy," he said, the words so quiet she had to strain to hear.

"Excuse me?"

"Tracking down their plans took almost no effort at all."

Paige frowned. It had taken them almost an hour just to find someone who had noticed the kids. "I don't follow."

"The woman at the crêpe stand saw them enter the metro station. The first employee we spoke to knew where they'd gone."

"They're eighteen-year-old kids, not government spies. Is it really so odd that they left a trail?"

Nick was quiet for a moment, then shook his head. "No, I guess not. We'll show their picture around the train station. Maybe someone saw them board."

Things started to click in Paige's brain. "You think the kids are trying to trick us."

"We can't rule out that they left a false trail just yet. By the time we arrive in Amsterdam, they could be in Italy." He rose and started pulling things out of his suitcase. "One way or the other, we'll find them."

"I'll fill Layla in on what's happening," Paige said.

"Pack whatever you can fit in a backpack. We don't want to deal with suitcases, especially if this ends up in a foot race."

A foot race. Paige hadn't considered that Evie and Ryan might run if they saw Paige and Nick.

"They wouldn't try and escape," Paige said, but she couldn't keep the uncertainty from her tone.

"They're two kids in a foreign country, scared and desperate. We have no idea what they're capable of, or what to expect."

"Comforting," Paige muttered. Fear made people unpredictable. Unpredictable usually meant stupid.

"Hey." Nick pulled her into a quick hug, resting his chin on top of her head. "It's going to be okay. I won't let anything happen to you."

The snakes in her stomach writhed in fear. "It's Evie and Ryan who are in danger."

"Right." He headed toward the bathroom and grabbed items off the counter. "Meet me in the lobby in ten minutes, and we'll leave for the train station."

Paige headed back to her bedroom on shaky legs. She'd never seen Nick look worried. It made this whole situation that much scarier.

In their room, Layla sat on the bed, her legs crossed and one foot bouncing rapidly. She looked up at Paige, her lips pursed.

"What did Don say?" she asked.

"He wants us to find the kids before we call their parents. Nick and I are heading to Amsterdam."

"He's not calling them now?" Layla's voice rose in alarm. "What if they were kidnapped? What if they're hurt? It feels irresponsible not to contact the police."

Paige closed her eyes and took a deep breath, trying to force the worried look in Nick's eyes out of her head. "Nick has everything under control."

"And what makes him qualified to deal with this sort of thing?" Layla demanded.

Paige focused on her suitcase, pulling out a pair of light-weight pants and a cotton T-shirt. "Don trusts him. And Don is our boss, so I'm doing what he says."

Was this how Nick had felt every time he avoided a question or answered with a half truth?

Layla rose, placing her hands on her hips. "I feel like there's something you aren't telling me. I'm worried, Paige. Something feels wrong."

"Let's hope you're wrong, and they just ran away for a romantic tryst." Paige zipped up her backpack and slung it over one shoulder. "Okay, I'm off. I'm sorry to abandon you and Tyler like this."

"We can handle the rest of the tour ourselves, no problem. It's Evie and Ryan I'm worried about."

"Me, too."

"Did Don give any direction on what to tell the rest of the group?"

"No." Paige tightened the arms of her jacket around her waist. "I guess keep it simple and vague. With any luck, Nick and I will be back by tomorrow night. We can figure out a better story once we know that Evie and Ryan are safe."

"Okay." Layla held out her arms, and Paige gave her a quick hug.

"I'd better go," Paige said. "Nick's probably already in the lobby."

"Be safe."

"We will."

"And call with updates when you can. Good luck."

Paige gave a fleeting smile, then disappeared into the hallway. Nick was waiting, a backpack slung over his shoulders and face impassive.

"Ready?" he asked.

Paige nodded, and they headed outside. The sun had fully risen, warming the air to a comfortable temperature. Paige knew it wouldn't last long—the sweltering heat of June would be out in full force soon enough. The fruit stand was now crowded with tourists buying apples, and the street in front of the hotel was congested with traffic. A moped zoomed between the bumpers, and a car horn blared.

"We'll take the metro to Gare du Nord," Nick said, setting a brisk pace.

Paige jogged beside him, taking two steps for everyone one of his. "What will we do when we get to the station?"

"Pretty much the same thing we've done all morning. Maybe someone will recognize their picture and confirm they boarded the train for Amsterdam."

"What if we can't confirm it?" Paige asked, her breathing growing labored. She stumbled over a crack in the sidewalk, but caught herself before falling. Nick didn't seem to notice.

"Then we'll hop a train to Amsterdam and hope for the best."

Paige stopped asking questions, struggling to keep up with Nick. They swiped their metro cards and ran onto the line heading toward the train station just before the doors closed. Paige steadied herself on a chair back as the train took off down the rails.

"What aren't you telling me?" Paige asked, glaring at Nick. "And don't lie to me. I know something's wrong—something more than Evie and Ryan running away."

The metro swayed around a corner, and Paige fell into Nick. He steadied her with one hand, his eyes far away.

"No more lies, Nick," Paige said quietly.

He nodded. "Something *feels* wrong. I don't know if there's a better way to explain it. After you've worked as an agent for a while, you get a sense about these kinds of things."

The panic was back, but Paige refused to give in. She had to stay focused. "Wrong how? Like Evie and Ryan really were kidnapped?"

"I don't think so." His eyes scanned the train car.

Paige looked around as well. There was a gentleman reading a newspaper a few seats over and three women in nun habits at the far end of the car. But there was no one close enough to hear their conversation.

"Amsterdam is what first caught my attention," Nick said. His lips brushed her ear, his tone barely more than a whisper. "That's where my last mission was—the one that went all wrong."

Paige sucked in a breath. "Do you think Evie and Ryan's disappearance is connected?"

"I don't see how it could be." He rubbed a hand over his eyes. "But I also don't understand why Don was so insistent you come with me. He knows I'm more than capable of taking care of this on my own. We used to work together."

Paige choked, then coughed. "You worked together *there*?"

"Yes. Don was an analyst, not a field agent. He only stayed for about a year, but we've kept in touch."

"I don't understand what you're saying." Paige shook her head, trying to make sense of everything. "Evie and Ryan are kids."

"I know. It's probably just a coincidence. But going back to that city has me worried." He grabbed Paige's hands, his eyes suddenly intense. "I need you to promise me you'll do exactly what I say while we're in Amsterdam. If I say run, you run. If I say hide, you hide. Got it?"

Paige nodded, struggling to breathe through the panic.

"Have you ever shot a gun?" Nick asked.

"No."

He sighed. "Okay. If there's time later, I'll give you a quick lesson. But it's better not to have a weapon that can be used against you, especially when you barely know how to use it yourself."

Black spots danced in front of her vision, and she forced herself to breathe. "You think I'll need a gun?"

"I don't know what to think anymore. But I'm going to keep you safe. You have my word."

She realized she was nodding over and over, like a bobble head doll. She forced herself to stop.

The metro pulled into the Gare du Nord station, and Nick and Paige got out. The room was crammed with tourists wearing fanny packs, young families with screaming children, and businessmen with pinched looks of annoyance. The cacophony of voices assaulted her senses, and she inched closer to Nick, overwhelmed.

"Where do we start?" Paige stood on tiptoes, struggling to see the signs. But people kept walking in front of her, blocking the view.

"That way." Nick pointed down a hallway.

Paige stayed close behind Nick, allowing him to blaze a trail through the crowd. The ceiling pitched high overhead, the glass panels letting sunlight filter through. Paige adjusted the backpack on her shoulders as her back grew damp with sweat. The room was muggy and hot, the buzz of activity confusing.

"There should be employees on the platform," Nick said, his head turned over one shoulder so she could hear. "Maybe musicians or artists who've set up shop for the day and saw something."

"Do trains to Amsterdam only leave from one platform?" Paige asked.

"They should," Nick said.

They were jostled onto an escalator. Paige peered down at the rows of trains below. Finding Evie and Ryan here was like looking for a needle in a haystack— labor intensive and probably hopeless.

Nick brushed a rough kiss against her forehead. "It'll be okay," he said, and she wondered who he was trying to reassure.

Paige saw a departure board at the bottom of the escalator and ran to it. A train for Amsterdam had left not even an hour earlier. Her shoulders slumped.

"I bet that was them," she said.

"Probably. It was a bullet train, too. Next one leaves in an hour." Nick pointed to the information desk in a corner. "If they did go to Amsterdam, we need to be on that next train. I think we should split up to try and cover the most ground. I'm going to talk to the ticket master. Why don't you talk to people who look like they've been waiting a while? The ones in a rush wouldn't have noticed anything, anyway."

"Okay," Paige said, her voice a squeak. She could already feel her heart pounding double-time in her chest.

He put his hands on her shoulders, looking at her with perceptive eyes. The green in them crackled, and she felt a rush of heat.

171

"You can do this. Be brave." He pointed to an information booth. "I'll be right over there."

Paige nodded, and Nick strode away. She looked around, overwhelmed by the sheer number of people.

Her eyes landed on a man sitting alone on a bench, watching as travelers streamed by. A people watcher. Perfect.

She took a deep breath, then walked over to him and sat down casually on one end of the bench.

"Bonjour," she said, forcing a smile that felt more like a grimace.

The man smiled back, his eyes friendly and warm. He wore a bowler hat and tweed jacket.

"Bonjour," he said, his accent decidedly English.

"You're British," Paige said in surprise.

"And you're American," the man replied. "What can I do for you?"

Paige pulled out her phone, hand trembling, and showed him the picture. "Have you seen either of these people? I'm chaperoning a tour group of high school students, and these two ran away. We think they took the train to Amsterdam."

"That's a bit of a bother," the man said. "No, sorry. I haven't seen either of them."

Paige deflated. "Can I ask how long you've been here?"

"Oh, an hour or two, I suppose. I like to watch the travelers."

"Okay." Paige rose, shoving the phone back in her pocket. "Thanks anyway."

"You might try that fellow right over there."

Paige followed the man's outstretched arm, and saw a musician across the platform. He leaned against a graffiti-covered wall, playing a guitar. She could tell his long hair was greasy even from across the room.

"He's been here since I arrived," the British man continued. "He does seem to watch the travelers intently. I've been keeping an eye on him in case he tries to pick anyone's pocket."

"Thank you," Paige said.

"Best of luck on your search." The man motioned to the musician. "Mind you be careful with that one."

"I will." Paige glanced back at the information booth. Nick was leaning forward, his muscles tense as he spoke to the employee inside.

She didn't need Nick. She could do this herself. Paige bounced on the balls of her feet for a moment, anxiety pooling in her veins, then forced herself to walk across the room. The musician did seem to eye everyone with an unusual amount of intensity. Her stomach curled itself in knots. Maybe he was a petty thief, like the British man assumed.

When she was only a few feet away, the musician caught her eye and grinned, revealing a decaying front tooth. Paige cringed but forced herself forward. He sang along with the music, wiggling his eyebrows up and down as he increased his volume. His voice actually wasn't half bad, even if his intense stare gave her the creeps.

"Bonjour," he said, still playing his guitar.

"Bonjour." She fumbled in her pocket for a five-euro note. She dropped it into his case, and it mingled with the other coins and bills.

His smile widened, and he continued to play.

"You're an excellent musician," Paige said, perhaps stretching the truth a bit.

"Thank you."

"Do you play here often?"

He raised a shoulder. "Two or three times a week."

Paige forced herself to keep going. She could do this—make small talk to extract information. "It must be a pretty good location, then."

"I get by."

She motioned to his guitar case. "Looks like you've been here a while already."

"Since the station opened for the day."

"Maybe you saw this couple, then." Paige held her phone out. The man leaned forward, and she caught a whiff of his overpowering body odor. Ugh.

He took the phone, and for one panicked moment, Paige thought he'd stolen it. But he merely zoomed in on Evie and Ryan's faces, his grimy fingers leaving a grease trail across the screen. "Yeah, I recognize them all right. The young couple that argued."

Too easy. Nick's words flooded back to Paige, and her hands shook as she reclaimed the phone.

"You're sure it was them?"

"Absolutely. They took the bullet train for Amsterdam." He pointed to the now empty rail line. "Barely made it to the platform in time. She didn't seem to want to get on the train, but they finally climbed aboard at last call."

Warning bells went off in Paige's head, but she forced herself to remain calm. "Did the boy force her to get on?"

He made a face, flashing the rotted tooth. "If he had, I would've helped her. No, it wasn't like that. She seemed reluctant, but they were holding hands when they got on."

So Evie had gone willingly, at least.

"Thank you. You have no idea how much help you've been." Paige tossed another five-euro note in the guitar case, then sprinted back to Nick.

He'd left the information desk and was walking toward her, his strides long and purposeful.

"That was less than informative," Nick said. "The woman thought she recognized the photo but didn't remember where she sold them a ticket to."

"They went to Amsterdam," Paige said breathlessly. "That musician over there confirmed it."

"How sure was he?"

"Pretty sure. They were fighting again. But I don't think Ryan's forcing Evie to come with him."

Nick blew out a breath. "Okay then."

"They've got more than an hour head start on us."

"That's okay," Nick said. "Once they get to Amsterdam, they're going to need cash. Hopefully, they use a credit card. And if they do, we'll be the first to know."

"Your friend is still tracking that?"

Nick nodded. "Yes. They made a withdrawal large enough for the tickets at an ATM somewhere in the station, right before that bullet train left."

Paige clutched the straps of her backpack, her palms clammy with nerves. "We're on the right track, then."

"I think so. Let's get back in line. Looks like we really are going to Amsterdam."

CHAPTER FIFTEEN

Nick couldn't stop his foot from bouncing as the French countryside raced past the train window. Three hours, and he'd be back in Amsterdam.

Well, you did plan on coming here in another three days, he reminded himself. But he hadn't planned on spending his time searching for missing teens, and he hadn't planned on having Paige with him.

"Why Amsterdam?" Paige asked aloud.

"What do you mean?" Nick asked.

"I mean, what made them pick that city over any other? I never heard either of them mention a connection to the Netherlands, or Dutch, or anything that wasn't American."

"There's quite the party scene in Amsterdam."

But Paige was already shaking her head. "You said that before, but it doesn't fit. Evie is fascinated by history, like me. And if she comes from an abusive background, why would she head for such a seedy city?"

"I don't know." Nick couldn't shake the feeling that somehow their disappearance was connected to his last mission. To Devin's death. Which was completely ridiculous.

"Okay, so where in Amsterdam?" Paige asked.

"Good question." Nick pulled out his laptop and booted it up.

Paige pointed to a sign above their head. "There's no internet on this train."

Nick smiled. Sometimes, he forgot what it was like to be a civilian. He pressed a few buttons, then opened an internet browser. "There's always internet when you're an agent."

Paige scooted closer, peering over his shoulder. "There has to be some kind of connection to this city. Family, maybe? A friend who lives there?"

"If there is, they never mentioned it."

"Check their social media," Paige said.

Nick was already pulling up the sites he'd perused earlier in their trip. "I didn't spend much time on Ryan's profile, but I've been through Evie's. There's nothing about Amsterdam on hers."

"Maybe they posted something today."

"They're not idiots."

"It doesn't hurt to look."

Nick nodded, pulling up Evie's account first. It was locked, the privacy settings not showing more than the name and picture.

Paige sank back against the seat, disappointment plain on her face. "Dang it."

"You're forgetting who you're with." Nick grinned, his fingers racing across the keyboard. Moments later, he was in to Evie's account.

"How did you do that?" Paige asked, her voice tinged with awe.

"Agency training." He scrolled through Evie's profile. It was mostly pictures of her and Ryan, with videos of cake recipes mixed in—nothing he hadn't already seen.

"She hasn't posted since they got to Europe," Paige said.

"I know. She was probably worried it'd upset her step-dad." Nick shook his head in disgust and clicked over to Ryan's profile. It was more robust, featuring pictures of Evie, but also his parents and little brother. Nick had scanned it before but hadn't bothered to dig for information. Evie was the one in trouble.

Or so he'd thought.

"They look so happy," Paige said. "Is he really giving that all up for Evie?"

Nick stared at a picture of Ryan with his dad. His father had the same lanky appearance as his son, and looked unexpectedly young—in his early thirties, though Nick knew that couldn't be right. The caption clearly labeled the other man as dad.

"They look just like each other," Paige said.

"Hard to believe that man's a millionaire," Nick agreed. "He looks so young." There was something about the man's eyes that bothered him. He sighed, leaning back in the seat. Worrying was making him crazy.

"What's Amsterdam like?" Paige asked.

A flash of Devin laughing as they shared a beer the night before the mission flashed into Nick's mind. He'd wanted to stay in the hotel room, studying up on the diamond cartel, but Devin had insisted they needed to unwind. "Kind of dirty. Lots of trash in the streets. But lots of history, too. The canals are beautiful, and there's a charm that's hard to describe."

Maybe if Nick had forced Devin to stay in, he'd still be alive. They might've stumbled across some piece of information that would've made Devin more cautious. Any variance might have created a butterfly effect that resulted in the bullet grazing Devin's arm instead of lodging in his heart.

"Nick?" Paige said quietly.

He shook his head, trying to banish the dark thoughts. "Sorry."

She brushed a hand through his hair, lingering where the longer locks caressed his collar. "It's going to be hard for you to go back to the city."

"Yeah."

"I'm sorry."

He patted her knee, forcing himself to take a deep breath and clear his mind. "Me, too."

They pored over Ryan's profile, digging deeper than Nick had before. Ryan frequently posted about working with his dad, and there were a lot of photos of the two together.

"Seems like they're pretty close," Paige said. She clicked right, and the picture of Ryan and his dad fishing transformed into one of them hunting together in Africa. "Geez, this family is loaded."

"Paying for Evie's trip must've been nothing to this guy," Nick agreed.

The next photo showed Ryan at his dad's office in New York, sitting behind the executive desk.

"He goes to work with his dad a lot," Paige said. "This guy is into everything. Look, he owns a chain of restaurants in Manhattan."

Ryan smiled back at the camera, an arm wrapped around Evie as they posed in front of a grill with a short Asian man in a tall chef's hat.

"It makes sense to diversify," Nick said. "It's pretty common for wealthy businessmen to try and grab a piece of every pie out there."

Paige clicked again. Evie posed in front of a glass display case, diamond earrings dangling from her lobes and a pendant hanging from her neck. The photo was over a year old, further back than Nick had gone in his previous research.

"Stop!" Nick said.

Paige paused, squinting. "*Just a little frosting for my girl,*" she said, reading the caption. "*One day, I'll run this place, just like my pops.* I guess Mr. West owns a diamond store, too."

Pieces fell into place like a jigsaw puzzle as Nick stared at the photo. At least a dozen engagement rings filled a glittering display case. Every single one of them had a center stone that had to be over a caret in weight.

Was Mr. West involved in the diamond smuggling ring?

He fit the profile—a wealthy businessman with multiple enterprises. Nick took the laptop back from Paige, shielding her view as he pulled up classified documents from the mission.

"Nick?" Paige said. "You're scaring me."

"It fits, but it doesn't," Nick muttered.

"The newspaper," Paige said suddenly. "That's was your mission, wasn't it? Diamond smuggling. You acted really weird when you saw that article."

"That's classified," Nick said automatically. He scrolled through the pages of information he practically had memorized, analyzing it in a new light.

"Do you think that Ryan's dad is somehow involved?" Paige asked, her voice doing that high, nervous thing that meant her anxiety was in full force.

"I don't know," Nick said. "Let me think for a minute."

Paige went quiet, settling back into her seat as she stared at him with wide eyes.

Even if Ryan's dad was involved, it made no sense. How would the crime ring have known Nick was in Europe? He'd only known himself a few days before and hadn't told anyone but his parents. How would they have even known he was part of the Amsterdam mission? His face had been hidden in shadows that night, and he'd retreated with the surviving team members less than five minutes after arriving. Nick hadn't been able to clearly ID anyone but Skeeter.

The countryside dissolved into three-story buildings and cobblestone bridges over canals. Tension built in Nick's chest as the train pulled into the station. He stored his laptop in his backpack, mind still spinning.

Paige's hand slipped into his and gave a gentle squeeze. "I'm not going anywhere," she said. "We're in this together."

He swallowed the lump in his throat and nodded.

"Where do we start?" Paige asked.

"I guess at the train station. Hopefully someone saw them leave and can point us in the right direction."

They stepped off the train, the humid air instantly making Nick sweat. He clutched Paige's hand, shielding her with his body as they made their way off the crowded platform.

Someone bumped against Nick, nearly knocking him off balance. The man kept his head down, a baseball cap shrouding his eyes. A paper fell from his pocket as he disappeared into the crowd.

"You dropped something," Paige called after the man.

Nick's blood froze in his veins. He snatched the paper off the ground and unfolded it. Somehow, he already knew what would be inside.

He stared at the address typed in all caps.

"What is it?" Paige asked.

Nick stuck the paper in his pocket and glanced around the room, making the motion casually. A man in a dark T-shirt leaned against the concrete wall, earbuds in but eyes watching Nick and Paige. Nick glanced away, feeling the reassuring pressure of the gun against his back. A woman with tattoos spider-webbed up her arms glared at them from the other side of the room.

"Nick?" Paige whispered.

He wrapped an arm around her, pulling her close as tension filled his body. He pressed his lips against her ear, pretending to kiss her, and whispered, "They're watching us. Act casual."

Her shoulders tensed, but she didn't look around. Pride swelled in Nick, but fear chased it away. He took a slow, steadying breath. He couldn't panic. He had to be an agent right now.

"Keep walking," Nick muttered.

If he told Paige to run, they might go after her. If he bolted and left her behind, someone might snatch her before he could circle back. He had to keep Paige with him. It was the only way to keep her safe.

"Where are we going?" Paige asked, her voice trembling.

Fear and determination battled in his chest for dominance. He tightened his grip around Paige.

"To a warehouse on a canal, near the outskirts of the city," he said. "I think we'll find Evie and Ryan there."

CHAPTER SIXTEEN

Nick stared back and forth between the tattooed woman and man with earbuds, heart thrumming in his chest. They were part of the crime ring, and they'd been sent to watch for him. He knew it deep in his bones. They were too carefully casual. Their gazes flicked in his direction too often.

How had they found him? Were Evie and Ryan really an elaborate trap to lure him here?

Nick hailed a cab just outside the station, all too aware that the man with earbuds and tattooed woman had followed them outside.

Nick held open the door for Paige, his eyes roving the street for signs of danger. Oh, how he wished Paige had stayed in Paris. Had he sentenced her to death by bringing her?

No. He would get her out alive, no matter what. He forced back the fear, locking away his emotions. Agent Nick needed to take control.

"Where to?" the cab driver asked in Dutch.

Nick rattled off the warehouse address without referencing the paper. The location had been forever burned into his brain two months ago.

"You speak Dutch?" Paige said, face pale. Trembles wracked her body. But there was a steely look of determination in her eyes that made him want to kiss her.

"And French, but I guess you already figured that out."

She shook her head, as though trying to clear it. "It doesn't matter right now. What is going on? I thought we were going to look for information at the train station."

Nick's heart lurched. Paige was so innocent—not cut out for an agent's life at all. She had no idea the paper had been meant for them. "The man who bumped into us? That wasn't an accident. There was an address on the paper. That's where we're going."

Her lips dropped in a frown, and his heart twisted.

"How do you know it was meant for us?" Paige asked.

He was leading a sheep to the slaughter. White-hot terror sliced through him as he contemplated losing Paige. She was his entire world. He needed her.

He couldn't lose focus. *Think like an agent,* he repeated over and over in his mind.

Nick pressed his lips against her ear, making sure the cab driver couldn't overhear. "Because I was at that exact address two months ago."

Her shoulders tensed, and she stared at him with terrified eyes. "Are you saying—"

He put a hand to her mouth, cutting her off. "Yes."

"So what does that mean?" she whispered.

"I don't know." He pulled the gun from its holster and checked the chamber, then concealed it once more. The cab driver was too busy cursing at a city bus to notice. "But I'm going to keep you safe."

"Are we headed into an ambush?" Paige asked, her voice high again.

He didn't say anything—just held her close, heart pounding erratically in his chest. He had to get that under control.

The cab pulled to a stop outside the canal Devin had died in. Brick buildings with pane-glassed windows rose four stories into the air. Paint peeled from the door frames. A bridge spanned the canal, a cargo-boat parked at the dock below.

Nick's palms were clammy with sweat, and he could hear his heartbeat in his temples. He gave the area a cursory glance, then opened the door and pulled Paige out, keeping an arm around her. He'd shield her with his own body if necessary.

He couldn't imagine a world that didn't include Paige.

He pulled out his gun and turned off the safety, but kept it pointed at the ground. The cab sped away, tires squealing against the concrete, as though the cab driver had sensed impending danger and was eager to get away.

Nick wished he could've sent Paige with him. But he couldn't protect Paige if he wasn't with her, and there was no guarantee she'd be safe without him.

"What now?" Paige whispered, her body shaking against his.

"They wanted us to come here," Nick said. "I'm sure they'll reveal the reason soon enough."

"Or they'll shoot us dead," Paige breathed.

Nick cringed. But no, the possibility was minuscule at this point. "If they wanted us dead, they could've done that in France. There's a reason I'm still alive."

And now, he'd brought Paige into this mess. Collateral.

The warehouse door opened, and a tall man stepped out. Nick flinched, his gun raised and ready to fire.

"Easy," The man held up a hand, face shrouded in shadows. The button-down shirt and expensive denim jeans looked out of place outside a warehouse.

"Show yourself," Nick commanded, his voice deadly.

The man lightly took the two front steps in a single bound, hands raised.

"Hello, Nick," he said, coming to a stop less than five feet away. "It's been a while. You look good."

Nick stared, his mind trying to take in the familiar sandy-blonde hair, dimpled chin, and lean physique. Nick's gun fell to his side, and the man pulled him into a tight hug.

Was this some sort of twisted dream? Surely Nick's mind played tricks on him.

"Devin," he choked.

Paige let out a gasp.

"I go by Daan now," Devin said, releasing Nick. "Helps me to blend in better. It's so good to see you again. Things haven't been the same."

A ton of bricks had fallen on Nick, and he wasn't sure how to sort through the rubble.

Devin was alive. Which could only mean one thing.

Devin had betrayed the agency. He was the mole.

Nick almost wished his partner was dead again. His chest hurt, and a scream built inside him that he refused to release.

Paige took a step forward, her tiny form shaking. Devin stared at her, one eyebrow raised. Nick grasped at the momentary distraction and reached inside his pocket, flipping the voice recorder on his phone. He shoved the gun back in its holster. Maybe Devin would forget Nick was armed.

Partners didn't draw weapons on each other.

"Where are Evie and Ryan?" Paige asked, a hint of shrillness entering her tone.

Nick grabbed her arm, pulling her toward him. She didn't know how to handle these types of situations. She didn't know what words might get her killed.

Devin was alive. Nick couldn't trust anything.

"They're probably enjoying a pastry at a coffee house," Devin said. His dark eyes glinted. "Mr. West will be very happy with their little performance."

The words were a punch to the gut. Nick tightened his grip on Paige, struggling to keep his face impassive. The information continued to click into place, like tumblers in a safe.

He didn't like the picture taking shape.

"Mr. West is the kingpin," Nick said slowly. "The kids were sent to keep an eye on me."

"And to bring you to the Netherlands, if it became necessary," Devin said. "It's not safe to stand here on the sidewalk. Come inside, and we can talk. Mr. West is very excited to meet you."

The kingpin was coming. A dull roar filled Nick's ear, and he struggled to keep his horror from showing.

Paige was here. The kingpin was coming.

They didn't stand a chance. He filed through a dozen possibilities, discarding most almost immediately.

Paige took a step back, her head shaking back and forth. She tugged desperately on Nick's arm. "Let's go," she begged.

Nick stared at her, despair sweeping over him. It was way too late for that. The kingpin wanted them for something, or they would've been killed long ago. Agreeing to the kingpin's demands meant a lifetime in debt to a criminal. Refusing meant certain death. Either way, he and Paige lost.

Devin pulled a gun from the waistband of his jeans and pointed it at them casually. Nick wasn't surprised. Why had he never considered Devin might have been the mole? His heart ached as his fury built.

He had loved Devin like a brother. Trusted him with his life. Nick stared at Paige, helplessness welling within him. Her face was white, her sapphire eyes huge and brimming with fear.

"I've already got the coffee brewing," Devin said. "It's rude to keep me waiting."

Nick eyed his partner, his mind working frantically. All bets were off now. He didn't know this Devin or what he was capable of.

Nick wrapped an arm around Paige's shoulder and urged her forward.

"That's better," Devin said, holding the door open for them.

The entryway opened into a wide hallway, brightly lit with florescent bulbs. Devin motioned to a door on the left, and Nick urged Paige forward. He felt her legs buckling and tightened his grip. *Be brave,* he thought, hoping somehow she'd get the message in his touch.

The room was no bigger than Nick's apartment kitchen in Virginia. A cheap laminate countertop ran along one wall. Scuffed white cabinets hung above the counter, and a small table sat in the center of the room.

"Sit," Devin said. He pulled three mugs down from a cupboard. "I must admit, you figured this out quicker than I anticipated. Mr. West won't be here for a while."

Paige sank into the chair, her eyes wide and frightened. Nick squeezed her hand, trying to offer reassurance. Why was the kingpin on his way? What could Nick possibly have that Mr. West wanted that badly?

Small, quick gasps were coming from Paige. Each sound tore through Nick's heart. He could feel her panic like a blanket descending over him. He had to get them out of here.

"Is Evie really being abused?" Paige asked, her words sharp and staccato. But she stared at Devin with unflinching eyes. "Is Ryan trying to protect her?"

Pride swelled in Nick at her brave questions, but he wished she'd stop talking before she got them both killed. Interrogating their captor—especially as a civilian with no training—wasn't a good idea. He squeezed her hand again, this time trying to send a message.

Devin laughed, placing a cup of steaming coffee in front of each of them. "That ingenious plot line was my idea. I knew Nick couldn't resist helping a damsel in distress."

"But the police reports," Paige said.

Devin shrugged. "No one's perfect. Her step-father's been on the lower rungs of the organization for years."

Nick's hand curled into a fist. The abuse wasn't just a plot line, of that Nick had no doubt. Evie was in even more danger than he'd originally thought.

"When did you go rogue?" Nick asked.

"About the time Don quit." Devin took a sip of coffee, one hand still holding his gun. "Mr. West pays better. I wanted to tell you so many times, but Don didn't think you'd ever come with us."

Don. Horror filled Nick at the blindside. He'd never considered he was involved, though now it was painfully obvious. After all, Don had known about Nick's feelings for Paige. And he'd been the one to insist she go with him on this suicide mission.

Maybe, if he created a distraction, Paige could escape. Was she thinking clearly enough to run if given the chance?

"There never was an attempted kidnapping last summer," Nick said with certainty.

Devin smirked, taking another drink. "Of course not."

"Why are we here?" Paige asked. She held Nick's hands tightly, knuckles white while her untouched coffee grew cold.

Devin addressed Nick. "Mr. West was concerned when you kept looking into things after my 'death.'" Devin made air quotes, gun still in hand. "That's when I convinced him we should bring you to Europe and figure out how much you knew. I suspected from the beginning it wasn't much, but I've missed you." He leaned forward, his eyes suddenly earnest. "It's a good life here, Nick. We could work together again, just like old times. Mr. West is willing to take you on. He's coming here to personally interview you, on my recommendation."

Nausea flowed over Nick, and he stared at Devin. Paige's fingernails dug into his skin.

"You're offering me a job?" Nick said, keeping his tone light.

Devin nodded, his eyes serious. "We'd be partners again. All you've got to do is impress Mr. West. You know, I've risen through the ranks quite quickly here. He trusts me—and my opinion—a lot. Don't let me down."

Nick didn't look at Paige, not wanting to redirect Devin's focus. *Run*, he yelled at her in his mind.

Devin had made one very critical error tonight. He hadn't taken Nick's gun. Their partnership ran too deep to ever suspect betrayal until it was too late.

"You know I've always been a straight shooter," Nick said.

"That doesn't mean you always have to be one."

Nick clenched his jaw, grinding out the words he knew could seal their fate. "I will never work for Mr. West."

Shock registered on Devin's face but was quickly replaced by anger. He raised the gun, pointing it at Nick. Paige screamed, her nails digging deeper. He wished she'd start running. Desperation clawed at Nick's chest, and he fought to keep his focus on Devin.

"I don't want things to end this way," Devin said. "There's still time to reconsider before Mr. West arrives. You and me had some good times."

"Don't you dare hurt Nick," Paige said.

Devin's eyes flicked to Paige for the briefest of moments. It was all Nick needed. He had his gun out of its holster and aimed at Devin in less than a second. Paige inhaled sharply, but Nick couldn't look at her— couldn't let himself be distracted.

"Why did you do it?" Nick demanded.

Devin laughed, the sound harsh and guttural. "Isn't it obvious? The work is easier, and the pay so much better. There's no red tape to wade through. The only rule I have to follow is kill or be killed."

"Why did you leak the false intel?" Nick pressed.

"I couldn't very well let us stumble upon the real plan. Besides, it was the perfect opportunity to escape. Mr. West agreed that it was too good to pass up. We'd both been searching for a way to get me out."

"Mr. West funds terrorists with those diamonds." Nick's finger itched on the trigger. How long until Mr. West arrived? He had to get Paige away from here before then, or they'd both be dead.

"Mr. West sells to the highest bidder," Devin said. "It's capitalism, pure and simple. The American dream in action."

Nick's heart thundered in his chest. His gun didn't lower, and neither did Devin's. If Devin shot him, what would happen to Paige?

He knew the answer to that question, and it was unacceptable.

"Pick the easy way," Devin goaded. "A life of luxury and ease."

"You know I can't," Nick said, fighting to hold the gun steady. To not look at Paige. Sweat trickled down his back, and the gun felt slick in his hand.

Devin sighed, then whirled, the gun suddenly pointed at Paige. The reason Don had made sure Nick brought her along became crystal clear.

A part of him had known it all along. She was insurance. They could make Nick do anything, as long as they had her.

Nick and Devin both fired. Devin's body jerked back, falling to the floor as a pool of blood appeared at the bullet entrance, right between his eyes.

Paige screamed, the sound bone-chilling. Nick rushed to her side, feeling numb. Blood poured out of her arm, and she stared at him in stunned shock.

She'd been hit.

Nick yanked off his shirt, his movements jerky. Just her arm. This could've been so much worse. It was just her arm.

Her head might be next. Mr. West or his hired thugs could still shoot Paige.

"You killed him!" Paige said, her voice bordering on hysteria.

"He would've killed you," Nick said. Later, he'd have demons to wrestle. He let the familiar numbness of a kill wash over him. For now, he had to focus on Paige.

She was still alive. He could still save them both.

He wrapped his shirt around her arm, and she let out a gasp.

"I'm sorry. So, so sorry." He grabbed Devin's gun and shoved it in his pants pocket. "We have to get out of here."

"What about him?"

"Mr. West will find him soon enough." They weren't out of danger just yet.

Nick pulled her to her feet. She swayed, and he wrapped an arm around her waist, steadying her. This was all his fault.

No. Agent Nick couldn't afford to think like that. Not right now.

He peered around the door, gun first and body on high alert. Clear. He walked swiftly from the room, supporting Paige's weight when she stumbled.

"This isn't how it's supposed to be," Paige said, rambling. "Did I seriously just get shot? This isn't my life."

"Shhh," Nick said. He opened the front door just a crack and peered out, then hustled Paige outside.

A car engine revved, and tires squealed around the corner. Nick pulled Paige back toward the warehouse with a curse.

Too late. Mr. West had found them.

The car jerked to a stop and the passenger door flew open. Nick threw himself in front of Paige, bracing for the bullet.

Paige would never get away. Not with a gunshot wound and crazed kingpin after her.

But it wasn't Mr. West in the driver's seat. It was Evie.

"Get in!" she yelled.

Nick made a split-second decision and shoved Paige inside the car.

CHAPTER SEVENTEEN

Paige slid across the gray leather of the back seat, the movement making her arm ache. Funny. She'd expected getting shot to be more of a white-hot pain. Nick's shirt was soaked with warm, sticky blood, making the fabric stick to her skin. She tried to hold her breath, the metallic smell making her ill.

"Evie," Paige said, vaguely aware that her words slurred together.

Nick slammed the car door shut. "Go!"

The tires squealed against the asphalt, racing toward the city center. Evie flew around a corner, nearly running over a pedestrian in the process. She cursed and swerved. Paige's arm hit the car door, and black spots danced across her vision. There was the white-hot pain. Paige struggled to catch her breath, tears filling her eyes.

"Oh my gosh, oh my gosh, oh my gosh," Evie said. "He's dead, isn't he? He must be, or you wouldn't have gotten away."

"Devin?" Nick asked.

"I don't know. Whoever wanted you here."

Paige leaned forward, stomach heaving. She fought back the bile. One moment Devin had stood there, face grim and gun raised. The next, he'd been shot between the eyes.

Nick had shot him. Nick, the guy Paige had passionately kissed in the moonlight. Nick, the man she loved.

Nick, the secret government agent who killed people as part of his job.

"What happened, Evie?" Nick demanded.

Paige let out a hoarse laugh. The world had ended, and nothing made sense—wasn't it obvious?

A tire jumped over the curb as Evie turned another corner. Paige closed her eyes, trying to blot out the stars dancing before them.

"I didn't know you, okay?" Evie said. "My step-dad's been close to the West family for years. At first, when they told us to lure you to Amsterdam, I thought, 'No problem.' But then we got to know you, and I started having doubts."

"Paige has been shot," Nick said. "We need to go to a hospital. I need to call the agency. Mr. West was on his way to the warehouse. He'll come after us—all of us. But if we can get in contact with the agency, I can keep us all safe."

Paige let out a shrill laugh. This was all so crazy. So unreal.

"I know." Evie's hands gripped the steering wheel tighter. "My step-dad will be furious when he realizes what's happened. Ryan, too."

"We can help you," Nick said.

Evie swallowed hard, staring straight ahead. "No. I won't leave my family, or Ryan. But I won't let them kill you two, either." She pushed on the gas, jetting through a red light.

"They'll come after us," Nick said. "They'll come after you."

Evie grabbed something from the front console and handed it to Nick. A thumb drive, Paige noted vaguely. Her brain was all fuzzy.

"Not if you come after them first," Evie said.

"What kind of car does Mr. West drive?" Nick asked, his voice even.

"I don't know," Evie said. "Depends. Whatever blends in."

Nick glanced out the back window, the tiny movement making the car bench shake. Paige hissed in pain.

"Where did you get this car?" Nick asked.

"I stole it from Mr. West," Evie said. "I didn't know what else to do. Ryan went to the bathroom, and I grabbed his keys and bolted. He's going to be so mad at me."

"We've got bigger problems than Ryan," Nick said. "Mr. West is following us. He probably tracked the GPS on the car."

A gunshot rang through the air. Evie screamed, swerving dangerously close to oncoming traffic. Another shot rang, and the back windshield shattered. Pebbles of tempered glass rained down around Paige, and her vision swirled sickeningly.

"Step on it," Nick said. He raised up, firing off his own shot before ducking down again.

"Where do I go?" Evie yelled.

Nick flicked a glance at Paige, his expression full of a thousand emotions she couldn't decipher. "Keep heading toward the hospital. Swerve as much as possible. He can't reload while driving, and he'll be out of bullets soon."

Evie blew through a red light, nearly getting T-boned by oncoming traffic. Paige blacked out, for how long she didn't know.

"You'll be okay," Nick said, his fingers running through her hair. "I think we lost him at that light. Hang on, Paige. It's just a flesh wound, and we're almost there."

"He's going to kill us," Paige said. Evie slid over another bump, and it was like someone stabbed a hot knife into Paige's arm. Tears poured down her face.

"No, he's not." Nick grabbed her face, staring intensely into her eyes. "We're both going to get through this, and we're going to be together. Do you hear me?"

Terror gripped Paige, but she tried to nod. She hadn't known she could be this scared and still breathing.

The car jerked to a stop, and Paige blacked out again. Rough hands firmly tapped her cheeks.

"Paige. Paige! We're here," Nick said.

Paige felt Nick's arms wrap around her and pull her from the car. She forced her eyes open, her entire body clammy with pain. An ancient brick building stood mere feet away.

The sliding doors opened, and a man in white scrubs rushed toward them. How odd. She'd expected medical personnel in Europe to wear something less familiar. The smell of blood was stronger now, and she fought back the urge to vomit. She'd die of embarrassment if she threw up all over Nick.

The man asked something in Dutch. Nick replied, his words rapid-fire. Why did his voice sound so far away?

A gunshot rang through the air, the crisp sound vibrating Paige's eardrums. She fell from Nick's arms and crashed against the cobblestone. She screamed as fiery lava consumed her arm, making it hard to breathe. Nick's gun glinted in his hand.

The man in scrubs dropped to the ground beside Paige, a stream of Dutch bursting from him. Cursing, probably. Paige felt like doing that herself.

After all they'd been through, this was how it'd end.

A man walked toward them, and for one panicked moment, Paige thought it was Ryan. But no, this had to be his father.

Evie dropped beside Paige, her eyes wide and terrified. "It's Mr. West," she whispered.

I love you, Nick, Paige thought frantically. Why had she let his secrets—his *necessary* secrets—come between them? He'd been doing a job. A job that would now get them both killed.

A cacophony of gunshots rang out. Paige's eyes were glued to Nick, watching him pull the trigger once, twice, three times. A scream caught in her chest, fighting for release.

"You've been a nuisance long enough," Mr. West yelled.

Another shot fired, and Nick dropped to the ground. Paige's scream burst forth, ringing underneath the awning.

No. Nick hadn't dropped to the ground—he'd rolled. Her entire body shook with adrenaline, and she could barely feel the pain in her arm.

Sirens sounded in the distance. Another shot.

Mr. West dropped to the ground.

Nick strode forward, gun straight out in front of him.

Mr. West's eyes locked onto Evie. His hand twitched on the trigger one more time.

Paige threw herself over the girl. Fiery heat tore through her leg with jagged bursts of pain—another bullet. Paige went limp, bright white stars bursting in her vision.

Two more shots fired. Someone screamed. Evie.

Paige blacked out. When she regained consciousness, she was lying on her back, staring up at an awning.

She glanced down. Deep crimson blood turned her jeans dark. Flashing blue and red lights pulsed across her vision, and the sirens were an angry snarl. They sounded off, somehow. Wrong.

"You're going to be okay," a rough voice said. Nick. She stared up at him, wanting to smooth out the lines on his face. But she couldn't make her arms obey the command.

Loud voices surrounded her, barking out orders in a language she didn't understand.

"Everything will be fine," Nick repeated.

She floated on waves. Loud beeps and urgent voices drifted in and out of her mind. She and Nick were kissing on a hilltop in Virginia. Holding hands as they strolled through the cherry blossoms framing the Lincoln Memorial. Complaining about another presidential motorcade clogging traffic. More beeps and urgent whispers.

And then, total silence.

The silence was nice. Comforting. But someone was calling her name, urging her to open her eyes.

Paige forced one eyelid open. Nick stared down at her, his green eyes filled with concern.

"Paige?" he asked.

"Where am I?" she croaked. Her throat was raw, and each word burned.

"The hospital."

He grabbed a water jug and helped her take a sip. The cool water bathed her throat, soothing the fire inside.

"Everything's going to be okay," Nick said. "Mr. West is gone. You're safe now."

Images flickered in her mind, along with a vague sense of fear. The pictures crystallized, and Paige gasped. The tiny movement sent pinpricks of agony licking over her entire body.

"Shhh," Nick said, smoothing the hair away from her face.

"What happened?" Paige asked.

Nick ran a hand over his chin.

"Mr. West showed up," Nick said. "Ryan found out that Evie had stolen the thumb drive and told his dad. At least, that's the story he's telling the police. Mr. West is gone. He won't hurt anyone ever again."

Paige blinked back the tears clouding her vision. Nick had killed to protect her. Twice.

"What happens now?" Paige asked.

Nick had aged ten years since they'd arrived in Amsterdam. His eyes were bloodshot, and green irises darkened as his pupils contracted. "Don is on the run. The agency is searching for him now. I doubt he'll be able to say hidden for long. There's a reason he was never a field agent."

"And the thumb drive?" Paige asked.

"I met with an agent and turned over that and my cell phone—I recorded Devin's confession. They've reopened the investigation, and I'll probably be taken off suspension very soon."

Off suspension. Paige closed her eyes, fighting back the panic. Off suspension meant back to work. And for Nick, that meant constantly risking his life.

She had to be optimistic. They'd survived Mr. West, which meant Nick could survive anything. If she was going to be an agent's girlfriend, she'd better get used to the fear.

"Evie and Ryan?" Paige asked, curling one hand around the hospital blankets covering her. Evie had risked everything to help them escape. If not for her, they wouldn't be alive.

"They've both agree to testify at the trial, and the agency wants them to go into hiding until after the trial. Ryan is devastated."

"I can imagine." Paige lifted her good arm, resting one hand on Nick's cheek. Tears filled her eyes, but she blinked them back. "I was so worried that you were going to die."

Nick turned his lips into her palm, kissing it. "I love you so much, Paige. If anything ever happened to you, it would be the end of me. I would fall completely apart."

She took a deep breath, then finally said it—the four little words she'd thought a hundred times but never had been brave enough to say. "I love you, too."

Nick's head snapped up. His eyes met hers, and she nodded.

"You've never said that before," he said.

"I know."

"After everything I've put you through—after the last twenty-four hours—you honestly still love me?"

She threaded her hands through his hair, the dark strands coarse and stiff from their adventures. "I do."

"That's the best thing I've heard all day."

His lips covered hers, warm and compelling. Paige returned the kiss with as much energy as she could muster, feeling the trauma of the past day start to heal.

Life with Nick would be far from easy. But she loved him, and his job was part of who he was. She was finally ready to accept him—all of him.

She couldn't wait to start the rest of their lives.

EPILOGUE

Paige stared up at the Eiffel Tower, awe filling her. Twilight filtered through the trees, and the tower glowed against the night sky, a beacon she yearned to explore. She put a hand to her heart, unable to stop smiling. This had been worth the wait. The only thing that would make it better was if Nick was here.

"It's so big!" one of the sophomores squealed.

"Dude, that's freaking tall," a boy said as he stared up at it. "Did people really try and jump from the top?"

Paige stuck her hands in her back pockets, feeling the pull of scar tissue on her bicep from the bullet wound. She'd been lucky—the wound in her leg had torn through some muscle, but with physical therapy, she'd made a full recovery. She'd worried that she wouldn't be able to handle all the walking required in

Europe, but a month into the job, she was doing just fine.

Evie sidled up beside Paige, a smile on her lips. "Was I like this last year?"

"Definitely," Paige said with a wink.

"Now I feel stupid."

"Don't," Paige said. "You had a lot going on."

Evie's eyes grew sad, and she looked away. "Yeah, I guess."

Don's trial had been held last month. The information on the thumb drive and Nick's recording of events had been enough that neither Ryan or Evie had been called up to testify. After Don's guilty verdict, the teens returned to regular life. Someone else had taken over the diamond smuggling ring, but Nick and his team had caused the organization a lot of trouble, and it was floundering.

Paige wrapped an arm around Evie's shoulders, giving her a squeeze. Evie's relationship with Ryan had been another casualty of the drama surrounding the diamond ring. Evie wasn't sure where Ryan was now, but she'd gladly accepted a letter of recommendation from Paige when Paige had suggested she join the tour group this summer. With Don gone, the company had been sold. The new owner had rehired Paige as soon as she applied.

One last summer in Europe—the summer Paige should've had last year. She'd had to quit the tour group after her injuries and had spent the rest of the summer convalescing in D.C., Nick rarely leaving her side.

Paige wouldn't be able to chaperone the tour group next year. Six weeks ago, she'd successfully defended her doctoral dissertation and earned her PhD. She'd begin teaching at Georgetown in September.

She wished she knew where Nick was right now. Every time he went on a mission, her heart lived in her throat. But being an agent was part of who he was, and she'd made her peace with it. She loved all of Nick— even the parts that kept her awake at nights, worrying for his life.

Evie took a step forward and raised her voice so the teens could hear. "Time to go inside. I've got the tickets for the elevator right here."

The teens followed after Evie, but Paige lingered, staring up at the tower that glimmered against the sky. There was a full moon tonight. It hung low in the clouds, bathing the entire world in its glow.

"Guess who?" a voice whispered in her ear.

Paige whirled, her hand automatically going to the weapon concealed in her waistband—the gun that was technically illegal for her to carry in a foreign country.

Nick. She dropped her hand and threw her arms around his neck, letting out a squeal. His beard was freshly trimmed, and his green eyes sparkled as she wrapped her arms around his neck, urging him closer.

Her hands threaded in his hair as her lips eagerly met his.

Two months was too long to be apart.

Nick brushed away the tears that rolled down her cheeks.

"What's this?" he asked.

"I just missed you so much."

He smiled, kissing her again. "The feeling is mutual."

"What are you doing here?"

"I believe I promised someone I'd take them to the top of the Eiffel Tower. I'm finally following through."

Paige laughed, linking her hands behind his neck. "How long are you here?"

His eyes clouded, the green deepening in what she'd come to know as his agent look. "A week this time."

It was never enough time. But she'd learned early on to not waste their time together worrying about when he'd be gone.

"Perfect," Paige said. "This tour ends tomorrow, and then I've got five days off. We can finally see London together."

"Sounds divine." A lazy smile turned up the corners of Nick's mouth.

"Can you tell me where you're going next?"

"Not this time." He squeezed her hand. "But by the time you return to D.C., I'll be back—this time, for good."

Paige's hands stilled on his shoulders. "What?"

"I finally got a transfer approved to a desk job. I'll be on the intel side of things from now on."

Excitement bubbled up in Paige's chest, and she forced it back. "But you love your job."

"I love you more."

She pulled away, shaking her head. "We agreed neither of us would change who we were for this relationship. I know sometimes I freak out over your job, but I'm getting better at it. I'm trying."

"Paige." He gently took her face between his hands. "I'm not doing this for you. I'm doing it for me. I don't want to start a family until I'm sure I'll be around to raise my children."

Paige's breath caught in her throat, and butterflies leapt to life in her stomach. "A . . . a family?"

Slowly, Nick sank to one knee. He withdrew a box and flipped it open. A single solitaire diamond on a band of gold was nestled inside the velvet case. Moonlight glinted off the stone, making it sparkle.

"It's conflict free," Nick said, grinning. "Promise."

"Oh my gosh." Paige put a hand to her mouth, tears pooling in her eyes.

"Paige Eldredge, I love you more than I can express. There is nothing I want more than to grow old with you. Will you do me the honor of becoming my wife?"

Paige laughed, throwing her arms around his neck. "Yes!"

He slipped the ring onto her finger and rose, wrapping her in a tight embrace. His lips covered hers, and she clung to him as he kissed her breathless.

Paige pulled back, and the clapping finally registered. She blushed, hugging Nick as she looked around to see dozens of people taking pictures and smiling, including quite a few of her students.

A whistle filled the air, and Paige smiled when she saw Evie cheering.

"I love you," Nick whispered in her ear.

She turned in his arms, kissing him once more. "I love you, too."

She couldn't wait to get started on their forever.

FREE EBOOK!

21,000+ DOWNLOADS. 150+ REVIEWS.

NOTHING SLOWS DOWN LOVE LIKE THE FRIEND ZONE...

Get started here:
http://smarturl.it/ClubVIP

WILL SAVING HER FAMILY FORTUNE MEAN LOSING THE MAN SHE LOVES?

Enjoy Layla and Tyler's thrilling romance!

Strike a Match: *Out of the ashes she might find true love.* When Kate's husband dies in a fire, she doesn't expect to fall for Taylor, the handsome firefighter who gives her the news. But past relationship fears and old habits threaten to tear them apart before they've even begun. Can the ashes of their pasts hold their happily ever after?

Meet Your Match: *Nothing slows love down like the friend zone.* Brooke's convinced all boys are trouble. Luke's a player who loves the thrill of the chase. Can a set of crazy rules keep these two safely in the friend zone?

Miss Match: *Playing cupid may break her heart.* With the matchmaking company she works for in decline, Brooke is desperate to sign Luke, her billionaire best friend, as a client. But Luke is more interested in capturing Brooke's heart. "This heartwarming, feel-good romance will leave you swooning and cheering for the characters as they fight for true love." -InD'Tale Magazine

Not Your Match: *Sometimes it takes dating Mr. Wrong to find Mr. Right.* Dating the wrong people has convinced both Ben and Andi that what they really want is each other. All that's standing in their way is a fake boyfriend, a jealous ex-fiancée, and being afraid to risk their hearts. "This pleasant tale will reward readers with the dance of life for a resounding happily ever after." - InD'Tale Magazine

Mix 'N Match: *Fire and ice aren't meant to mix.* Zoey and Mitch couldn't be more opposite. One passionate kiss has convinced them they'd never work. But three weeks in Paris could change everything. "The witty dialogue and the emotion that slowly enraptures the reader makes this book a gem." -InD'Tale Magazine

Mistletoe Match: *A kiss shouldn't be this complicated.* When animal rights activist Michelle kisses a mystery man underneath the mistletoe at a holiday party, she's horrified to realize he's the new marketing director of the pharmaceutical company she's trying to destroy due to their nasty habit of animal testing. Can one impulsive kiss be the foundation for a happily ever after?

WELCOME TO
Sunset Plains, Oklahoma

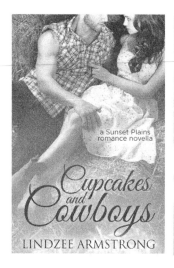

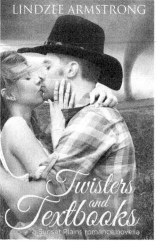

DIVE INTO THIS DRAMATIC WESTERN ROMANCE SERIES!

Cupcakes and Cowboys: *He's everything that broke her heart.* Cassidy wants two things—to make her cupcake shop a success, and to forget that her fiancé traded her for the lights of Hollywood. When Jase—best friend of her ex and A-list actor—shows up at the ranch to research an upcoming role, forgetting is the last thing she can do. Can Jase convince her he's really a country boy at heart?

Twisters and Textbooks: *Some storms can't be outrun.* After the death of her parents, chasing tornadoes is the only thing that makes Lauren feel alive. Each storm gives her the adrenaline rush she craves, but it can't make her forget Tanner, the country boy she left behind in Oklahoma. When a tornado brings the couple back together, Lauren and Tanner are caught up in a cyclone of emotions neither is sure they want to escape. Can they weather the storm of their past, or will they let it consume them?

OTHER BOOKS BY
LINDZEE ARMSTRONG

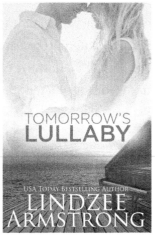

Chasing Someday: *Three women. One struggle.* When a school book drive brings Megan, Christina, and Kyra together, their uncomfortable secrets soon come to light. Can they overcome their mutual heartache, or will they allow infertility to tear them apart? "With a smooth pace and plot, and plenty of emotional depth, this is a must read for contemporary fans!" -InD'Tale Magazine; recipient of a Crown Heart review!

Tomorrow's Lullaby: *Falling in love just got complicated.* When Sienna McBride placed her baby for adoption, she never dreamed that two years later she'd find herself falling for someone who resents his birth mom for not keeping him. Will Sienna choose to live a lie, or trust Aaron with the truth?

First Love, Second Choice: What happens when you impersonate your identical twin sister to score a date with your long-lost high school crush?

ABOUT THE AUTHOR

 LINDZEE ARMSTRONG is the *USA Today* bestselling author of the No Match for Love series, Sunset Plains Romance series, and Kiss Me series. In case it wasn't obvious, she's always had a soft spot for love stories. In third grade, she started secretly reading romance novels, hiding the covers so no one would know (because hello, embarrassing!), and dreaming of her own Prince Charming.

Lindzee finally met her true love while at college, where she graduated with a bachelor's in history education. They are now happily married and raising twin boys in the Rocky Mountains. Traveling is one of their favorite activities! Lindzee has visited eleven different countries (most of them in Europe) and more than thirty-five states.

Like any true romantic, Lindzee loves chick flicks, ice cream, and chocolate. She believes in sigh-worthy kisses and happily ever afters, and loves expressing that through her writing.

To find out about future releases, you can join Lindzee's VIP reader's club through her website at www.lindzeearmstrong.com.

Made in the USA
Monee, IL
15 September 2021